CROSSING THE
BRIDGE OF SIGHS

CROSSING THE BRIDGE OF SIGHS

SUSAN ASHLEY MICHAEL

TWIN
OAKS
PRESS

ISBN-13: 978-0-9844354-7-0

First Edition

Printed in The United States of America

Twin Oaks Press
twinoakspress@gmail.com
www.twinoakspress.com

Cover and Interior design
By Art Growden
artgrowden.com

Cover photo by
George Peters

In loving memory of Robert Michael

1

Del senno di poi son piene le fosse.
The graves are filled with hindsight.

As the *vaporetto* made its way along the Grand Canal, an underlying rush of sighs and murmurs blended with the lapping of water against ancient foundations. Haunting whispers that reverberated along the damp alleys seemed to be calling to me, one voice growing more insistent than the others. What was it saying?

"Marco!"

Without a thought about consequence, my injured heart leaped to respond.

"Po-lo," I murmured.

And before I could draw my next breath, a thick cloud of moisture gathered and wrapped itself around my chilled body like a heavy cloak. I brushed at the dense mist, willing it away, and told myself to ignore these beckoning shades and to focus instead on the zigzagging path of the *Numero Uno* as it continued along the Grand Canal's parade of glittering palaces.

Some say that Venice was created when an angry goddess tossed a bowl of sweets and it landed here in the lagoon, scattering shards of crystal and candy. I saw my life as a shattered candy dish and couldn't imagine anything beyond its brokenness. When Bernie first entered my world, I envisioned him as a noble Saint Bernard come to rescue me from the cold, empty vastness of my days. But he hadn't come to rescue me at all, only to use me as a cover, and finally to desert me, running off to become a dot in the distance, a period at the end of a long sentence.

Swooping into my field of vision, a boatman in a striped shirt and pressed pants turned his heart-shaped face toward me, and as he worked the long, single oar of his gondola with ease, I felt my own arms aching with the strain of having hauled Bernie's stolen luggage. Time to get rid of it, I realized, so grabbing both our bags, I debarked at the next stop and summoned the gondolier.

"Angelo," he said, by way of introduction as he pulled up, stowed the luggage, and offered his hand.

"Take me way out into the lagoon," I said, gesturing.

His eyes held a question, but he answered in a pleasant tone, "*Va bene.*" Negotiating the choppy green water with grace, he hummed a barcarole, its rocking rhythm mimicking that of the boat. The tune lulled me into a more peaceful state until we reached deep waters and were quite alone. Then, recalling my mission, I grabbed Bernie's bag and flung it open.

"Into the drink," I yelled, my voice unsteady. "My husband's a no good cheating bastard, and I'm getting rid of anything to do with him!"

"*Scusa?*" Angelo said, his almond eyes widening as I plunged into the jumble of clothes, grabbing the first thing I could get my hands on. A silk scarf, the distant smell of aftershave and Bernie's smooth neck. Hugo Boss? No, Calvin Klein. I tied the scarf in knots so tight my knuckles turned white, and when it hit the water, it floated away like a glob of spilled paint. I raised my hand to wipe a tear, but my fingers now smelled of early mornings in bed. Back into the bag I went, this time pulling out a cashmere cardigan that matched the blue of Bernie's lying eyes. I tossed that, too, along with pricey pants and tailored shirts. Into the lagoon they all went. And finally, I heaved fistfuls of premium cotton underpants—the ones that hugged his shapely butt. When they refused to sink, I was overcome with fury and frustration, and made a move to grab the oar from Angelo. I wanted, more than anything, to poke at the revolutionary seamless pouch—and give a twist.

"*Che pazza!*" Angelo yelled, managing to hold the oar out of my reach.

The sleek vessel rocked wildly as I screamed, "Stab them! Do you hear me!"

"Madonna!" the gondolier moaned, shaking his head.

With a growl, I tugged at my wide gold wedding band, tossing it into the littered water. My eyes spilled with tears, and the lagoon's surface turned from choppy green to a timeless gray waterway of thousands of damp, shifting pages torn from discarded books, blurry-inked letters, diary entries, tragedies and stories that had promised a happy ending. Then I sobbed and sobbed until Angelo, his expression softening, offered me his neckerchief. He studied me for a moment as I mumbled "*Grazie*," and dabbed at my eyes. Then he tipped his straw hat, red ribbons fluttering, and answered "*Prego*," with an inflection that sounded more like "Pray, go!"

"The Accademia," I said, and we headed for the Canal and the graceful wooden bridge. When we reached the bank, he helped me disembark, and I tried to return his neckerchief. But Angelo shook his head no, so I handed him one of my business cards instead. He looked at its logo, TRAVEL LIGHT, and grunted.

"*Arrivederci*," I said. See you around.

"*Addio*," he replied. Not likely. Then he pushed off and disappeared among the throng of watercraft.

2

Non tirare i remi in barca.
Don't pull your oars into the boat.

I was searching for my friend Josie's rental, an ochre house draped in ivy, not far from the small square where the San Trovaso workshop was located. In the distance a whistling craftsman, busy with plane and glue, was working on an upended gondola, and I was struck by the thought that if something as rare and precious as this watercraft could be repaired, then maybe there was hope for my tattered, upside-down heart.

As I rounded the corner, the passionate tenor tones of Pavarotti singing *Nessun Dorma* soared from the open window of an ivy-covered house, the words both lifting me and making me grateful for the anonymity that Venice offered. *Il nome mio nessun saprà!* No one will know my name.

But when I reached the green lacquered door, I hesitated. Josie knew not only my name, but everything about me. College roommates at Smith, we both settled in the Massachusetts seaside town of Newburyport, me to do my travel writing and Josie to dabble in antiques and to rehab a rambling Victorian in the center of town. I braced myself for the advice and cajoling that she was bound to serve up with her tea and crumpets. After all these years, Josie continued to be a free spirit who, unperturbed by life's tragedies, just kept plowing ahead. I didn't know if it was resiliency, wisdom, or pure unbridled energy, but she wasn't one to spend time licking her wounds. The word "contemplative" was not to be found in her dictionary. Josie was a friend, yes, but also a force to be reckoned with.

And there were times I had caught her in lies. White lies, she called them, convenient corner cutting, an expediency, she said. It was an irritating habit with no treachery involved, no harm done, and reflecting on our friendship over recent years, I was pretty sure she had outgrown her light, white lies just as she had abandoned her heavy, black mascara. These days, her great dream was to open a café back home, her goal in Venice to gather recipes and learn some cooking tips from the Gritti Hotel's renowned Chef Nicolò.

I straightened my shoulders, took a deep breath, and rang the doorbell. Soon my friend appeared, looking the same as ever: unruly red hair, lively green eyes, and mismatched outfits worn with unstudied ease. Today, a floral bib apron, polka-dotted Mary Quant, and black shoes so pointy she could crush the smallest spider in a corner.

"I've been *so* worried about you after your call," she said, rushing to give me a long hug. Then in a gentle voice, "Here, let me take your bag." She led me, heels clicking, through the living room to the guest bedroom, with its high ceilings and pale blue walls. Scooping up an embroidery hoop and basket of colored threads that lay on a soft chair by the lace-covered window, she stowed them in the maple armoire before pulling out a worn luggage rack. A buzzer went off in another room.

"The timer," she said.

Then, a second buzz.

"And that would be Boccaccio's imitation of the timer."

"Boccaccio, a new boyfriend?"

Josie laughed. "I'm parrot-sitting. It's part of the deal."

I followed my friend to the sunny kitchen where the scent of lemon zest lingered in the air, and a beautiful African Grey paced sideways on his roost.

"He's a sly one," she said to me. Then in baby talk, "Aren't you, Boccaccio?" The bird ruffled his gray feathers, mimicked the tinkling of her charm bracelet. "He's no trouble, though. And to show her gratitude, the *contessa* gave me a major discount on the place. Seems the bird was her husband's and outlived him." The parrot flicked his red tail. "He could outlive us all."

"Perhaps," croaked Boccaccio.

"No cognitive powers, my foot!" Josie said, tossing some flax seed into the large cage. "Did you see that documentary on crows, how they perch at an intersection and drop walnuts in front of oncoming cars? When the light turns red, they strut along the crosswalk and pick up the nuts, all shelled and ready to eat. Pretty clever."

Josie slipped her hand into a quilted mitt and removed a pan from the oven, the comforting smell of warm polenta and toasted almonds filling the room. "But not nearly as smart as my little sweetie-pie here."

She dusted the pie-sized cookie with confectioner's sugar, placed an almond beneath its center, and tapped the surface with a demitasse spoon, breaking the crunchy disc into serving sizes.

"Here," she said, handing me a piece. "It's a variation on the *fregolata*. I'm collecting as many regional recipes as I can."

"For your café."

"Getting to be more of a reality, I want you to know."

I had the impression that the room held an echo, until I realized it was the parrot, matching my every bite with a loud, chewing sound of his own. Once he had my complete attention, the feathered genius recited a phrase in Italian: "*Non tirar i remi della barca.*"

"Never give up," Josie translated, popping a piece of cookie into her puckered, lipsticked mouth. "In Treviso, they bake these so hard they have to break them up with a mallet. This one's for my neighbors," she said, arranging more raw dough in the pan, sprinkling it with sugar and nuts, and sticking it in the oven. Then she smacked her lips and let out a "Soooo . . . " Hands on her hips, she looked me over. "I'll make us some coffee, and you can tell me what's going on. I didn't expect to see you for a couple of weeks. And you were so upset yesterday when you called from Paris, I couldn't make out . . . "

My voice trembled as I described the events that had brought me early to Venice and to Josie's doorstep. "We were at the Père Lachaise Cemetery, finishing up a piece on romance and tragedy."

"Hmm."

"It was the usual: Bernie doing the photos, and me taking notes. Except that an eerie feeling crept over me when we came to a pair of marble figures at the entrance of one of the vaults. As if Bernie and I might be those two lonely figures, about to enter the world of the dead."

From the cupboard, Josie took two mugs, one with a handle in the form of a flamingo, the other with a basket-bearing burro. "Flea market finds," she said, sliding the beast of burden toward me. She set a pot on the burner where a blue flame flickered.

"We had an hour before the gates opened to the public, and went our separate ways, planning to meet at the tomb of Héloïse and Abélard."

Josie put the steel filter in place, dumped in ground coffee, screwed on the top.

"I stopped by Victor Noir's grave."

"The bronze dude with the shiny crotch?" Josie said, reaching for spoons from the drawer.

"I know, why did I bother? I was rubbing his bulge when the gatekeeper's wife showed up with white mums. She looked me up and down and said, 'You hope that you make a baby, eh?' Then she patted her big belly, gave Victor a kiss, and put the flowers at his feet."

"A token of appreciation," Josie said, helping herself to more cookie.

"You know, Josie, I never would have married Bernie if he hadn't sworn he wanted children. And he was so attentive, everywhere except in the bedroom."

The pot began to hiss, and when Boccaccio followed suit, Josie poured our coffee.

"I'm forty-five, a carrier of old eggs. That's what I was thinking at Victor Noir's. Anyway, I visited more graves, and then, in the distance, I heard Bernie's voice coming from the direction of Oscar Wilde's tomb. I don't know . . . I thought maybe he had met up with the gatekeeper's wife, too. But something made me hesitate in the shadows of an old chestnut tree. I watched as Bernie picked up one of the scattered notes and read from it, 'One should always be in love and that is the reason why one should never marry.' He laughed as if that were the most hilarious thing." Tears spilled, dampening my cheeks. "I felt a stab in my chest, and then I heard a man's voice. Tittering."

Biting her lip, Josie handed me a box of tissues.

"It was Eric, from the Champs-Elysées. We'd been to his boutique earlier in the week for Bernie's birthday gift, a lambskin jacket with a hefty price tag.

I noticed Eric standing too close to him while they admired their reflections in the mirror. Then he adjusted a shoulder. Stroked a sleeve."

I reached for a tissue and blew my nose.

"And here he was in the cemetery, dressed head-to-toe in black leather with the fit of a glove. Or condom. Stinking of patchouli, and saying, 'Marriage, a mistake that can be easily corrected.' So sleek, svelte and gelled."

"One big Eric-tion," Josie said, narrowing her eyes as she slurped her coffee.

I cringed when Boccaccio, who had remained silent until now, called out, "Eriction!"

"Then everything went into fast forward. I heard Bernie say, 'I love it when you talk dirty.' I saw him push Eric hard against the stone and kiss him on the mouth. Then Eric turned his back to Bernie, and dropped his pants."

"Oh-mi-god."

"I let out a gasp, but they didn't notice. When I turned to leave, I tripped. I tried to steady myself, but my bag fell open and everything went flying. There was this horrible snap, and my first thought was that it was the sound of my heart cracking open. But it was my cell phone hitting the corner of a tombstone. It shattered, pieces everywhere. I *had* to get out of there, but I was frantic to find the memory card. I got down on my knees, sweeping the ground with my hands, feeling for it in the dirt, the grass, but nothing. So I left it there, with that last call from Mom and Dad." I dabbed at my swollen, aching eyes.

"Oh noooo, Claire." Josie sniffed. Having forgotten to set the timer, she pulled the overdone cookie from the oven.

"I took a taxi back to our hotel, threw my things in my carry-on, and then figured, what the hell, and packed Bernie's, too. His fancy-schmantzy crewnecks, his fruity French underpants . . . "

"Forget 'off the beaten track,'" Josie said, finding a small hammer in her junk drawer and slamming the rock-hard cookie; "this was Paris through the back door!"

"I thought Bernie was the real thing, but he turned out to be . . . "

"A fucking fag," she muttered, under her breath.

I felt my face crumple, and from its cage, the African Grey screeched,

"Fucking fag! Fucking fag!"

I grabbed another tissue before trying the coffee. Bitter.

"So you must have had an idea . . ."

I shrugged, avoiding her eyes. "The early years were okay. We tried to get pregnant, but then we were so busy with our work. And he brought home flowers, chocolates, and read aloud to me in bed. And we kind of forgot about it."

"Having a baby."

"Well, yes. And about going through the motions to make a baby."

"You didn't have sex."

"Not for a while."

"Uh-*huh*." She tapped the long slender leg of her ceramic flamingo.

 "I found a website for women who wonder if their spouses are gay."

"Women who wonder," squawked Boccaccio.

"Well, you're not wondering now." Josie brushed some crumbs from the table into her open hand.

"Honestly, it makes no difference whether it was a man or woman," I said. "The point is Bernie's a liar and a cheat, and here I am, left with nothing." I couldn't begin to describe how alone I felt, with no one to dream about me, wait for me, long for me. I was nobody's *numero uno*. And truth be told, by the time I got around to searching for that website, it was obvious that something was very wrong. There was no lipstick on Bernie's collar, but there were his late nights working out at the gym, his styled hair, and lately, a shelf lined with depilatory creams.

"There's no sense beating yourself up," Josie said, dropping the crumbs into the cage. "It's not your fault."

I gave my chipped cup a sorrowful glance before taking a last swallow of coffee.

"Well, why don't you take a look at these," she said, pushing an open newspaper toward me and tapping her glossy fingernail on the page of personal ads. "You could write one of your own." This is so Josie, I thought, as she pulled a blank card from her rickracked pocket, scooted her chair next to mine, and started composing an ad. "What have you got to lose? Let's see, sexy travel writer . . . "

"*Sexy?*" the parrot repeated, adding its own inflection.

"It's way too early for that, Josie. Really. I'm still in shock."

"Someone to lead you in the actual footsteps of Petrarch or Picasso," she continued. "Sensible, organized, loves movies."

I shook my head.

"You're right, it needs sparkle. How about, 'Guaranteed to fascinate.' I mean, look at you—still hot." She smiled as she scribbled, "Beautiful traveler would love to accompany you to your favorite café, then a movie. Funny, appreciative, down-to-earth."

She looked pleased until, with a furrowed brow, she reached over and tugged at my hair. "Better lose the braid, though. It makes you look uptight."

"Please, Josie, forget about it. Do us both a favor and use this to line the birdcage." I pushed the paper in her direction.

"Okay, okay." But she was still singing and dancing like she always did just before she went off the deep end. "And your clothes." She gave me the once over. "All black. You're like Chekhov's Masha, mourning her life." She grew silent for a long moment before patting my hand. Her eyes softened.

She knew how I grieved for my parents. Ever since that December morning five years ago, on their way to pick me up and take me out for my birthday, their lives were cut short on the slick New England roads, taken by a drunken driver. My mother and father, gone. The memory returned like a lion's paw, hollowing out my chest in one ravaging swipe. Josie knew she had to be careful where she stuck her pointy shoes, *and* her nose.

"I mean it," I said, "stop this or I swear I'll never speak to you again." Because this whole scene reminded me of that fatal moment twelve years ago when Josie returned from a trip to Boston, all charged up about running into a guy who had been in her Italian class. "You have *got* to meet him, Claire. He travels on photo assignment, mostly in cities because he says he loves the urban whirl, and he's *gorgeous.* You two would be a perfect match." And that's when Bernard, former Amherst College participant in the five-college consortium, stepped into my life. Maybe I shouldn't blame Josie. But still, I do.

"Don't give up on yourself. I'm thinking you'll get a whole new slant on

Venice this time," she said, oblivious. This *che sarà sarà* attitude of hers really got under my skin. "By the way, I met someone named Ethan last week at an auction, and he's joined my cooking class." She poured us more coffee. "Want to see what I picked up at the lingerie shop?" Visions of silky thongs, peek-a-boo v-strings, and lacy garter belts danced through my head.

While Josie prepared lunch, I found *Rear Window* on TV. Jimmy Stewart, with his leg in a cast and a camera pressed to his face, spying on his neighbors. And Grace Kelly telling him, "Start from the beginning. *Dimmi tutto* . . . . Tell me everything you saw, and what you think it means."

I had been dazzled by appearance and charm, the prospect of the perfect man, and with our combined genes, the promise of the perfect babies we would parent. And here's what I think it means: Women should come equipped with some kind of radar to help them avoid all this heartache. And they should be cautious. Look at Josie, impulsive Josie, always in too much of a hurry to fix everything—with Gorilla glue. Who knows how things would end up in her reckless hands? Nothing would line up; nothing would work. The craftsman restoring the gondola didn't use some slapdash approach. He took his time and mended with care.

That night over dinner, when I tried to convince my friend to ease up, she flashed me a smile and nodded, but I could see that her mind was skipping way ahead. "You need to come to class with me tomorrow morning. You'll *love* Chef Nicolò, and you'll meet Ethan."

Exhausted, I helped her clean up, gave her a hug, and as I made my way to the guest room, Boccaccio called to me. "*Sogni d'oro!*" Golden dreams. That night I dreamed of my wedding ring, tossed into the lagoon, spinning slowly and settling into the mud, a circle of gold surrounded by other lost and forsaken relics.

Long before the first tourists began trickling over the bridge, Josie and I left the house. Church bells chimed as schoolchildren hustled past us, lugging backpacks. We swerved around small groups of Venetians gathered to gossip and talk politics.

"This is why they call it a living room city," she said.

"Everything but a sofa and coffee table," I said, glancing at posters taped to the ancient walls.

"Wouldn't be a stretch. Some older women in my neighborhood drag their chairs out every afternoon and sit for hours knitting and keeping track of things. Now that they know me a little, they share their favorite recipes." As we crossed the bridge, she added, "Hard to believe, but one of them told me her parents had never set foot on the mainland and, in fact, hadn't in all their lives crossed the Grand Canal. Can you imagine? Market, pharmacy, church, friends. Their little neighborhood met all their needs. And at the end of the day, they'd find a bench on the promenade, hold hands, and watch the sun set over the Giudecca Canal."

I tried to imagine the utter contentedness that the couple must have felt to remain rooted back there in Dorsoduro.

We soon reached the Gritti's russet façade and passed through the gold-rimmed doors to the lobby. Thick, lush oriental rugs arranged on the marble floor softened each footfall. On one of the rich silk damask walls hung a portrait of the sixteenth-century doge who built the palace.

"Let's grab a little something before we get to work," Josie said, reaching for a croissant from the table in the Club del Doge. "Made by the chef." Her eyebrows jiggled with delight as she took a bite and offered one to me. "Aren't they the best ever?"

As we entered the hotel's spacious kitchen, her new love interest, Ethan, greeted her with a hug. His aquiline nose had suffered a break, and a silvered scar ran across one blond eyebrow, lending character to his otherwise flawless face. He handed us our toques, stiff with starch, and as Josie pulled his strawberry-blonde hair back into a short ponytail, he flashed me a smile.

Gathering around the massive butcher-block island, we were surrounded by aromas of the strong local salami and the lingering sweet and sour scents of Arabic specialties. Opera music playing softly in the background brought to mind the whispering ghosts that had called to me from the alleyways. But when Chef Nicolò, a solid man in his sixties, greeted me warmly, those thoughts quickly evaporated. After he offered instruction on the various dishes, we all got to work. When I wasn't peeling and chopping, I assembled simple recipes like the cornmeal cookies.

"*Zaeti*. Venetian for 'little yellow ones,'" said the chef, stopping by briefly to check on me.

As I kneaded the gritty dough, my deep sadness drifted away. And the one time I stopped, immobilized in thought, Josie nudged me with her elbow and handed me a cup of rum-soaked sultanas. "Don't dwell," she whispered.

When lunchtime approached, Chef Nicolò gathered us for a demonstration on how to slow-cook onions. "Simmer over a low flame for twenty minutes, then add a dozen anchovies—more if you want zing," he said, scooping the syrupy sauce onto thick pasta called *bigoli*.

"Forget about hand-blown glass and feathered masks," he said, a strand of silver hair escaping the wide band of his pleated toque. "You will find the most fabulous palette in all of Venice at our own Rialto market. The fruits and vegetables, *fantastico*! And now . . . " He grabbed some ripe tomatoes from the counter, tossed them in the air and caught them. "*Gioia!*" His blue eyes sparked. The dimples in his cheeks deepened. "We cook for pure joy, juggling the flavors," he said, letting the tomatoes roll into a fry pan of sautéed onion and minced garlic, and breaking them up with his fork.

"*Allora* tear the *basilico*. Never cut. We don't want it to blacken. Add it to the goat cheese, roasted garlic, and olive oil. Then surround the little hills of cheese with tomato, one serving for two people." As everyone paired up, Chef Nicolò brought his plate to me and handed me a fork. Sharing the dish, we talked about his favorite recipes, my favorite cities, the wife he lost to cancer, and the accident that claimed my parents' lives. I didn't mention Bernie. He wasn't worth talking about, and besides, I was afraid of breaking down. As I left class that afternoon, Chef, as if sensing my sadness, rushed up to take my hand in both of his, and kiss it.

Josie spent most nights with Ethan at his place, and when the loneliness crept in, I was glad for the parrot's company. I offered him mixed seeds and berries until he warmed up to me, then opened his cage door and took him out to perch on my arm. We worked on proverbs. Boccaccio had "A bird in the hand" pretty well mastered when there was a knock at the front door, followed by "Hel-lo?" I returned him to his cage and hurried to the door, to find no one there. When I came back puzzled, Boccaccio danced excitedly on his perch, and repeated, "Hel-lo? Hel-lo?" This knock-knock prank became my nightly cue that he was ready for a head scratch.

No longer weighed down by a cell phone, I grew meditative for long stretches. The loss of my memory card continued to nag at me, but I had carried it around for years and listened to the message so often it had become more a self-flagellation than a comfort. Along with suffering the loss of my parents, I bore the guilt of the survivor. The irrational voice in my head repeated, "You should have warned them about the roads. You might have saved them." There was nothing left to do but tuck my parents' last message—*We love you!*—into the folds of my heart, where it would stay forever.

When the week had passed, I called the Pensione Accademia where the desk clerk assured me that my room was waiting for me. My last morning with Josie, she slipped a gift-wrapped package into my bag and, as she and I paused at the open door, Boccaccio called from the kitchen, "Don't be a stranger!"

"I don't know what I would have done without you," I said, giving my friend a big hug. "I mean it, Josie. Thank you!"

"No problem. You know I'm always here for you," she said. "I wish you hadn't smashed your phone."

"I'm easy to find. Here's my itinerary."

"So, tomorrow," she said, studying the paper I handed her, "it's dawn at Saint Mark's Square."

"Never fails to inspire."

"You know, I'd love to have a picture of you there."

"Easy enough." All I had to do was hold my camera at arm's length, paste a smile on my face, and pretend to be caught in an exciting moment.

Fregolata

1 cup blanched almonds
1/2 cup granulated sugar
7 tablespoons unsalted butter, melted and cooled
2 egg yolks
2 teaspoons lemon juice
Grated zest of 1 lemon
1 teaspoon vanilla extract
1/4 teaspoon almond extract
1 cup fine yellow corn meal
3/4 cup all-purpose flour
Pinch salt
1/4 cup blanched almonds, chopped
2 tablespoons brown sugar

Preheat oven to 350 degrees F. In a blender, grind almonds with 3 tablespoons granulated sugar to a coarse powder. Add remaining sugar and process to a very fine powder.

Transfer to a large mixing bowl and beat in the butter. Add egg yolks, lemon juice, zest, and vanilla and almond extracts. Mix until blended. Add cornmeal, flour, and salt to almond mixture and stir until the dough comes together. Butter a 10-inch tart pan with a removable bottom. Spread dough in pan, using fingers to distribute dough to the edge. Sprinkle with the chopped nuts and brown sugar.

Bake 5 minutes. Reduce heat to 300 degrees and bake 45 minutes longer, until surface is pale golden brown. Cool completely on a rack. To serve, place a whole almond under the center of the cookie and rap the top with a demitasse spoon to break into serving pieces.

If you lose track of time, have a mallet on hand.

3

Le ore del mattino hanno l'oro in bocca.
The morning hours have gold in their mouths.

The Pensione Accademia hadn't changed since the fifties when Kate Hepburn stayed here during the filming of *Summertime*, and there was no trace of the "churlishness" mentioned by one of the Brits in his travel book. In fact, a friendly porter sprinted my bag up the forty stairs to my room where arched windows offered a view of a rose garden, a stone cupid, and the Grand Canal.

I was working on a piece about the Madonna and, specifically, the various ways she was portrayed by the Venetian masters. I planned to meet with Gianni, an art restorer from Naples. He had been helpful with past projects—the lions of Venice, the architecture of the palaces—but during my last assignment, covering Chihuly's massive glass installation, Gianni had acted less than professional, too touchy-feely. I shrugged off any reservations, though, left my things in the room, and walked the short distance to his shop where a sign on the door read, *Chiuso.* Through a smudged windowpane, a startling satyr in hand-blown glass danced, his erection caught by a ray of light. As I peered more closely through the glass, I saw that deities of the woods and mountains exhibiting various stages of excitement were scattered throughout. The shop was so altered—cluttered and dark—that I checked the number on the door before leaving a note.

For the time being, I put Gianni out of my mind and, with no ring tones from my lost cell to tear me from my reveries, I enjoyed the pedestrians' lyrical phrases that fell on my ears like a medley of Verdi arias. I was grateful for the way my life had quieted, and I would defend my right to let nature take its course.

As the city grew dark and the first lights blinked on, I returned to my room, changed into flannel PJs, and spread out the tools of my trade: map, journal, pages torn from various Venice guidebooks. Limit yourself to carry-on, I advised my readers, maximum weight eighteen pounds, total combined dimensions forty-five inches. As for clothing, stick with black and white. And try to include an item that makes you feel at home, for example, a photo of a loved one. Except that I had no photo to prop on my night table. I placed my neck pouch on the dresser and arranged my toiletries in a row, and that calmed me in the same way an airline's divided serving tray always did.

Ignoring the twinge in my chest, I opened the package from Josie. Ever since the loss of my parents, she's been on a campaign to supply me with soothing textiles while satisfying some need of her own. So we both have lighthearted pillowcases covered in pink poodles, dancing ladybugs, smiling snow people and, now, a map of the world.

As I set the alarm for five, I noticed a red speck that refused to budge, a tiny heart my friend had satin-stitched on Venice's location. Finally, I flicked off the light, gave the pillow a final squeeze, and drifted into the dark.

It was still dark when I took the stairs to the ground floor hoping for some coffee, but the dining room was empty and silent. Goaded by Josie's remark about resembling a widow, I pulled a rose from the porcelain vase in the foyer, stuck it in my hair, and headed out the door, imagining myself instead a mysterious *signorina*. Crossing the bridge, I followed yellow signs that read "per San Marco" and marked a path that led down crumbling alleys and across squares redolent of marsala and fresh-baked bread. I fought an urge to run into the Gritti, bid Chef good morning, and beg for one of his flaky croissants. Instead, I hurried along to the piazza, reminding myself that sunrise waits for no one, and reached Europe's grandest drawing room, with nothing less spectacular than heaven itself for a ceiling. It was me and a few groggy pigeons, off-hour and off-season.

The closed cafés gave no hint of yesterday's crowds—not a dirty napkin, not a cigarette butt—in a city more than a thousand years old. I helped myself to a couple of wicker bistro chairs from the stack beside the Florian's barred door and lugged them out into the piazza where I could catch an unobstructed view of the domed basilica and its four charging horses.

When a line from Lord Byron sprang to mind—*Before St. Mark still glow his steeds of brass*—I recited it to the empty square, then tried to set my bag on the chair next to me and was more miffed than startled when it met with some resistance, as if already claimed by some invisible force. In a blink of the eye, a phantasm appeared, a man with dark curls and long-lashed eyes of a changeable gray. He wore a soft white poet's collar with a loose silk scarf and a black embroidered jacket.

"Love affairs," began Lord Byron, summoned, I supposed, by his own words.

"No, thank you," I said, giving my bag a decisive shove. "'Mad, bad, and dangerous to know.' Just what I *don't* need." Then, alone once again, I shimmied back in my chair to stretch my legs and wait in the quiet peculiar to this city on water until dawn reached over the basilica, outlining it in gilt and pink. Finally, a rush of light washed the piazza's sweeping expanses, shifting everything from sepia to full-blown blush.

In that instant, the silence broke with a flutter of wings followed by the sound of footsteps on the marble floor behind me. A lanky man with black, wavy hair appeared, flashed me a smile, hesitated, then pulled a thermos from his pack. "*Scusi, vorrebe bere un caffé con me?*" His accent was obvious.

"I'm American, too," I said. His eyes, the rich brown of Venetian espresso, caused a tingling in the back of my neck, an inarticulate longing in my chest. Pull yourself together, I told myself. He's what—maybe thirty-two, thirty-three?

"Well, that makes it easy," he said.

"Here, have a seat." As I moved my bag, I noticed that my hand shook, that I hadn't bothered to do my nails, that I was five, no, ten pounds overweight.

"Coffee?" he asked. A dark mole high on his right cheek accentuated the depth of his eyes. "I'm Max." His handshake was strong but not overpowering, and it transferred a sensation like static electricity that nipped my palm. That's when he pulled a copy of my latest book from his bag. "I don't want to miss a thing, and the beating heart of Venice," he said, extending his arms as if to embrace the entire piazza, "tops the list."

Beating heart. I couldn't believe he was quoting me. He took my nervous laugh as a sign of agreement and nodded in the direction of the basilica.

"That's . . . " My voice faltered.

"Fantastic, isn't it? A raft of dreams rubbed with a ripe peach." His voice was a baritone that resonated in my breast as he quoted me once again. If I were a house, all my windows would be rattling. I hesitated to break the spell by informing him that it was *my* book he was waving around. He tore a hunk of warm bread and handed it to me.

"Picnics . . . "

"Yeah." He wiped his hands on his jeans. "You don't need a reservation." Oops, he's switched now to my annoying rival Rick Steves, PBS travel guru. And the next line out of that luscious mouth was bound to be, "You're guaranteed a table by the window."

It was high time to complete my sentences and identify myself to this traitor, but instead I came out with a somewhat lame, not entirely true, "Picnics are forbidden here in Venice."

"No way." He studied me for a long moment, and gave a shrug. "Well, rules were meant to be broken." His collar was frayed, his camera case battered, and a speck of red jam glowed from his upper lip. I fought an urge to lick it off.

"First time here?"

He nodded, his black hair spilling over one eye. "I'm in art history, and I've seen a million slides of all this. But to actually be here stirs the heart." He brushed something from his face. A tear? *O that I were a glove upon that hand, that I might touch that cheek!*

"It's all strangely familiar," he said. "Not from having seen slides, nothing like that. In fact, you know what?" He squinted at me. "*You're* familiar. I just can't . . . "

I'd waited too long and felt foolish. I reached for the book and pointed to my picture on the back cover.

"I can't believe it," he said, blushing. "I've been carrying this everywhere. Sorry, I didn't recognize you." His eyes moved from the jacket to my face. "It's just that you look so serious in the picture." He hesitated. "Unhappy."

"Ouch."

"All I'm saying is you're much prettier in real life."

I melted. His eyes strayed to the stack of chairs by the café and he wiped the jam from his mouth.

"*The Chair at the Florian,*" he said. The air stilled around me and my body stiffened. "Did you ever read it?"

"Never heard of it," I lied, struggling to swallow a mouthful of coffee.

How could I possibly forget the sad little story that had been on Smith's required reading list? What was he suggesting?

"You can't put your life on hold," he said, gazing into my eyes.

"That's the story?"

"Basically, yeah." He moved closer, setting his cup on his knee. I picked up the faintest smell of rosemary. "A woman makes love with a stranger here at the Florian," he said. "On a chair, after hours. It's the one happy moment in her life, so years later she comes back to steal a chair."

"As a souvenir."

"But the night watchman catches her and makes her put it back." His gaze shifted toward the low domes of the basilica. "It's all sinking," he said.

Three inches a decade, maybe more. But my thoughts lingered on the lonely middle-aged woman returning home without passion, or furniture.

We sat together for some time, Max balancing his cup on one knee.

"I've been holding my breath," I said, "waiting for your cup to fall."

"What difference would it make in a city where bricks topple and towers tumble?"

I glanced up at the campanile, a replica of the one that had collapsed in 1902. "It's true. Every day Venice loses something. A nose from a bas-relief, a folio, a fresco."

"Then there's no better place on earth for learning to let go," Max said.

Still, I held onto my cup with both hands. "So where are you staying?"

"In a synagogue," he said. Those eyes.

"That's unusual."

"A friend of mine has connections in the Old Ghetto. The apartment's modern, but as soon as I step into the shadowy courtyard and damp alleys, time shifts. As if the scrim between past and present turns transparent."

"I know," I said. "A distant call from across a canal can pull you into the past." I felt so in tune with what he was saying, but "Take me, I'm yours" wouldn't work. Or would it?

Max got up, blotting out the sun, and brushed crumbs from his lap. When I looked up to meet his eyes and the rose slipped from my hair, he scooped it up in a single sweeping motion and kissed it.

"Your turn," he said, pushing the flower against my lips, the feel of softest silk collapsing. Then he stuck the rose in his buttonhole and glanced at his watch. "Crazy early, I know, but I'm meeting a friend before her first class."

While I fumbled for a business card, he jotted his number on a sticky note and posted it on my sleeve.

"Do me a favor? My friend asked for a picture of me here," I said.

And before I could get the camera out of my bag, he said, "Big smile," and used his own. Then he gave a quick wave goodbye and hurried off, calling, "Catch up with you later."

I watched as he moved with effortless long strides across the patterned floor of the square to disappear down Marzaria de l'Orologia with *my* rose and *my* picture. But as the morning bells rang from the campanile, I reminded myself that Venice is a village where everyone meets again sometime or other.

A fluttering of wings. Max? No, a pigeon arrived, eager for the day's first offerings. I took a last look at the two empty chairs and left the café to stroll beneath the portico that skirted the square. Workmen in orange jumpsuits had appeared to collect trash and cart it to green barges that waited on the canal. Two *carabinieri* in deep blue coats and two-cornered hats were on their way to observe the hoisting of the flags of the Republic. I continued along the circuit of arcades, stopping to admire a torso-shaped vase of hand-blown glass with two curved lines that ran down the front suggesting an unfastened blouse. I took the sticky note from my sleeve, smiled, and put it in my bag.

The tearoom at the Quadri Café, rich with pastoral paintings covering its walls, offered a velvet window seat where I could linger to watch the square outside fill with Venetians, tourists, and the vendors who set up their carts to sell packets of corn for the pigeons. Once the waiter took my order and left, I noticed the lamp dim and a slight movement flicker in the corner of the room. It began as a wispy outline and, slowly as a Polaroid print develops, a figure materialized. First, a pale face, probing brown eyes, straight nose and finally, a pencil-mustache. Marcel Proust, author of the longest book I've ever read, gave me a little nod, sending a whiff of tired shoes and wilting lilacs my way. "The real voyage of discovery," he said, "consists not in seeking new landscapes but in having new eyes."

After my parents passed away, I could feel them hovering around me as I waded through deep sadness, and then, when I least expected it, a wave of grief would build and crash over me, knocking me down. One morning not long after their deaths, I caught a blurry glimpse of the two of them on a crowded sidewalk. Another day, there they were: translucent, holding hands as they admired a shop window. My parents always held hands—sitting side by side in bed watching TV, sharing a meal at their favorite restaurant. And in the car, my Dad drove with one hand on the wheel and the other curled around my mother's tapered fingers.

It occurred to me that Byron and Proust were members of the distinguished circle of souls said to reside here in the city, their wisps lingering like fragments of old film. From that first day on the *vaporetto*, they sensed my distress. I was beginning to see myself as the ghosts must, a grieving middle-aged woman too reserved to have sex on a chair with a waiter perhaps, but still in desperate need of company.

Monsieur Proust peeled off his pearl-gray kid gloves and leaned in my direction to murmur, "My dream has become, incredibly, but quite simply—my address." Then he crossed his legs and devoted full attention to his Madeleine cake and cup of tea. Out in the piazza, someone played a muffled "As Time Goes By," and when the music faded, so did Proust's eyes and nose. His mustache floated briefly in mid-air. Then that too was gone, along with his gloves.

Soon my waiter waltzed in with a silver tray that held a croissant and cappuccino, a crystal goblet of ice water and packets of butter wrapped in foil, tossed in like little gifts. He set these before me, along with a pair of paper napkins delicate as butterfly wings.

4

Per San Martino, cadono le foglie e si spilla il vino.
For Saint Martin's Day, the leaves fall and one drinks fine wine.

The Ducal Palace is often compared to a large pink birthday cake, but there's really nothing sweet about it. It was not only the seat of government, but also a law court where the Terrible Ten meted out their justice. A penetrating chill settled in one huge, silent gallery after another as the doges, grouchy men in red robes and peculiar hats, stared out from their portraits, tracking me all the way to the gloomy Council Chamber where a tour guide stood, a yellow umbrella hooked on her arm.

"Accusations, such as the one against the painter Veronese, were dropped into the lion's mouth," she explained to her group, thrusting her umbrella in the direction of the beast's face carved into the far wall, its lips parted in a nasty snarl. "He was accused of sacrilege in his *Last Supper*." She paused for effect. "But the artist simply renamed his work and kept his head." The guide smiled, as if claiming a personal triumph.

Her voice faded as she herded her group toward the far end of the room where they congregated before an expanse of dark canvas. "After stabbing an opponent to death on the tennis court—he *hated* to lose—Caravaggio fled to Sicily and slept with a knife under his pillow. Later, the poor young man missed his boat home and collapsed on the beach, his rolled paintings clutched in his hands.

"And then there are the countless Madonna paintings, but here in the Ducal Palace Our Lady must share each canvas with one genuflecting doge after another."

Leaving the Chamber, I went on my own to find Tintoretto's *Mary and Child*—the mother and son airborne and surrounded by saints and chubby angels, with Doge Nicolo da Ponte assuming the usual position.

When at last I reached the enclosed Bridge of Sighs—*A palace and a prison on each hand*—I pressed my forehead against the gritty scrollwork that offered prisoners a last view of sky and lagoon. If only I had studied Bernie the way that tour guide had studied the masterpieces. But I was too busy poring over maps of Paris, London, and Beijing to note his occasional scowl, an arched eyebrow, and the way his eyes avoided mine.

Below, I caught a fractured, flickering view of a gondolier bent to the oar, moving as if he and the boat were one. Some people sailed through life that way. Like Max, so free and easy, balancing coffee cups on his knee.

I left the Bridge of Sighs, wandering until I reached the elegant promenade of Strada Nova where a group of admirers gathered around a rosy-cheeked infant propped in a Perego carriage. The sight of them awoke in me a longing to feel the weight of a child against my shoulder, to inhale the baby's sweet smell. The infant opened and closed its little fist while the mother adjusted a fleece blanket. Overhead, a clothesline squeaked when a woman with a knob of gray hair leaned from a second-story window, lowering a wicker basket.

"*A bèl bèlo*," she called in velvety dialect to the girl and boy below. "Easy now. One for each of you." I was reminded of Emily Dickinson in the upstairs window of her Amherst Colonial, lowering her gingerbread and scribbled notes.

"*Grazie, zia! Grazie tanto!*" the children answered, taking their twined packages from the basket. A dozen steps away, customers were pouring out of the neighborhood Boscolo Bakery carrying similar packets. I stood in front of the window display contemplating its assorted nut-adorned pastries. At the base of one tray overflowing with gondolier's kisses, someone had scrawled, "A woman who expects a gondolier to be true has hams over her eyes." Glitzy bakeries were often highlighted in guidebooks for their edible replicas of Ferragamo footwear, but there were good reasons why the windows of the Boscolo were marked with a thousand fingerprints.

A young boy stood so close that I could smell the itchy dampness of his wool coat, the clover and comfrey of his shampoo. The two of us admired one spectacular cookie that took the form of a man on horseback. It was a foot high and decorated with curlicues of frosting, studded with chocolates, and sprinkled with silver shot. His mother, her cropped hair red as an autumn leaf, dipped her head to hear what the boy was whispering in French.

"Saint Martin," she answered in English. "The Roman soldier who cut his cape in two, sharing it with a beggar."

She looked up at me then with her acorn-brown eyes. I returned her smile before letting my gaze drop to her child's face, then to her swollen belly. Doubly blessed. But my attention was pulled away from them when, in the superimposed reflection of pedestrians on the bakery window, I caught a familiar slope of the shoulders, a shock of black hair. My heart skipped when I realized it was Max, moving along with the crowd, close enough that I could turn and touch him. But as I was about to say hello, an elegant blonde with an expensive haircut, dressed in a pink Versace fitted sheath, hooked her arm through his. When he took her hand and brushed it with his lips, a mixture of disbelief and jealousy swept over me and I brought my fingers to my own lips, remembering the rose we had both kissed earlier that day. The blonde pulled a large iron key from her purse and I imagined that it must open a private gate, one that they would close behind them with a decisive click as they disappeared into a dark alley.

Traveler's Tip: Don't fall for a stranger.

The young boy continued to stare at the elaborate cookie, his look of longing mirroring my own.

"May I buy that cookie for your son?" I asked the woman.

"Really? That's so very kind of you." When I introduced myself, she patted the boy's shoulder. "This is Etienne. And I am Nicole."

The three of us stepped inside the bakery together, and when the signora handed Etienne the Saint Martin confection wrapped in cellophane, he leaned into my side, giving me a shy half-hug that nearly brought me to tears. Nicole explained that she was sorry to rush off, but they were meeting her husband at the National Library. We said goodbye and as they joined the pedestrians on the walkway, Etienne turned and mouthed, "*Merci.*" Then he took his mother's hand and they melted into the crowd.

Alone once again, I scolded myself for my silly romantic fantasy about Max. Probably triggered by the wanton Lord Byron, I thought, as I consoled myself with a half-dozen gondolier's kisses and a thick strawberry yogurt drink. In the end, all men were gondoliers, weren't they, navigating their way through life. Well, there were no longer hams over *my* eyes.

Queuing up at the San Marcuola stop, I noticed a man with cropped sandy hair dressed in an expensive looking sweater and jeans, his high forehead and strong chin hinting at intelligence and determination. His blue eyes held my gaze, and there was a hint of a smile on his full lips. My age, I decided, and touching my mouth in a flirty way, discovered to my horror I was sporting a pink mustache. I searched for a tissue in my bag and turned to the nearest bench, wanting to could crawl under it.

Finally, the growling waterbus pulled up, clanging against the dock. While the Venetians took seats inside to read their papers and chat, the rest of us remained outside to watch the palaces glide by, their window ledges dotted with geraniums intended to discourage any lingering mosquitoes. I squinted at the Titian sky where I counted six, no, seven shades of blue. Then I grabbed a bench in front of the captain's wheelhouse window to wait for the Ca' d'Oro to appear.

"House of gold," said a tourist as the palazzo's decorative façade came into sight.

"*What* gold?" said her companion.

"Worn away long ago."

Reaching for my camera, I remembered Bernie's instructions to divide the frame in thirds, vertically and horizontally. Then, for dramatic tension, place the subject off center. When the two figures on the balcony of the adjacent pink palazzo came into focus, I saw that it was Max and his companion. I pressed the camera to my face like a mask and took a picture of them as Max turned toward the waterbus. What was it Bernie always said? Oh, yes. "Don't ever let your brain trick you into thinking that your subject is closer than he really is."

In *Rear Window*, injury granted Jimmy Stewart license to spy on his neighbors. Well, I was injured, too, and now I felt ridiculous, spying on a man I had just met. A man ten years younger, who wore jam on his lip, stuck notes to strangers' sleeves, rattled off quotes from a travel book as if the words were his own. When the waterbus stopped to pick up more passengers, our captain pounded on the window with his fist, gesturing for me to sit down so he could do his job.

In the movie, Jimmy, armed with a curious mind and a pair of binoculars, spends his time gazing out his apartment window into those of his neighbors, studying their private lives. Like him, I was in the healing stage and reminded myself to take everything slowly, a little at a time. No more overwhelming situations. What I needed was to visit a museum, to absorb the containment of a whole world on a sheet of canvas. Or better yet, within a three-dimensional enclosure. I knew someone who could turn chaos to order, box it up and top it with a sheet of glass. And he was close by.

5

Chi trova un amico trova un tesoro.
One who finds a friend finds a treasure.

Most visitors are dazzled by all the usual twentieth-century greats at the Guggenheim Museum, a sprawling, white *nonfinito* that sits on the bank of the Canal like a forgotten layer of wedding cake. But unlike most, I gravitated to Joseph Cornell's series of box constructions. This armchair traveler allowed me to observe time and space undisturbed by outside forces. Displayed on the walls of a narrow corridor, each of his shadow boxes held ephemera and souvenirs from an opera, a ballet, or a bubble blown from a clay pipe, holding each safe forever, preserved and intact.

I wanted to see a work called *The Pharmacy*, but the docent in the Dutch boy haircut explained that the medicine bottles filled with tulle, feathers, shells, and other prescriptions for a wounded spirit had been placed in storage. Permanently. Her mascaraed eyes said, "Tough."

Overhearing our conversation and probably reading the disappointment in my face, a statuesque woman with snowy hair swept back in a flawless French twist commiserated. "*Peccato.* I love that piece." The terrier in her embroidered tote cocked its head and whimpered. "A dose of pure joy to treat what ails us." The woman studied my face. "Isn't that Cornell prescribes?" The terrier squirmed.

"Why, yes." The artist puttered for years with his collection of shadow boxes. One of them contained mummified waves, mini-coastlines, and twenty-one compasses with needles pointing every which way, and seemed to say that we may be navigating unpredictable waters, but we're all in the same boat.

The woman crooned, "*Stai brava, Zola!*" She offered her hand, the diamonds in her antique ring sparkling. "I'm Daniela. And you are . . . " I was about to introduce myself when she continued, "the travel writer, I know. I'm in publishing, too. I've seen your likeness on the dust jacket of your books which, by the way, I enjoy very much."

"Thank you," I said, pleased to be recognized. I acknowledged her terrier's extended paw with a gentle shake.

On the wall before us, a box held a stuffed parrot surrounded by playing cards, suggesting a theme of fortune telling and games of chance. "I'm going to make a quick trip to the ladies' room," she said. "When I return, why don't we have lunch together?"

"I'd love to," I said. "I'll find us a table."

As I watched her walk away in her heels and Armani suit, a raspy voice spoke up from the box construction, as if the parrot had been biding his time.

I moved in closer, my breath fogging the glass.

"Endless possibilities," he whispered. I pictured the labeled shoeboxes of paraphernalia that Cornell kept stored in his basement in Queens.

"Joseph?" A timid bachelor, Cornell ventured regularly into Manhattan to collect the materials for his art.

"Trinkets from Woolworth's, pie and coffee at the Waldorf Automat . . . " the parrot was saying when a wistfulness swept over me at the mention of the Automat. As a student, my mother had lived in Manhattan and eaten there, amused that the cafeteria's food selections were displayed in diminutive coin-operated compartments, one dish behind each glass door. "They looked so precious!" she said. "Of course, the whole place was a kind of a schmaltzy café done up in Pepto-Bismol pink where we would spend hours reviewing philosophy notes or translating Catullus."

"That's what inspired my boxes, the Waldorf!" Joseph's voice adopted a lilt. "Always remember . . . "

I pressed my ear to the glass, to make out Cornell's final words.

"The key to transformation is juxtaposition with . . . "

"Yes?"

" . . . the unexpected."

From the parrot's beak to my ear.

An imperious Chinese woman in a red ankle-length coat swept past, accompanied by a tall blond man in a black coat, fur-trimmed hat, and red scarf. They gave the impression of having walked off the lid of a lacquered Russian box. As they made their way to Peggy Guggenheim's former bedchamber, I went in the other direction to pick up a couple of postcards at the museum store, but stopped in my tracks. A salesman was in the process of unlocking the display case where a familiar woman in pink pointed to a heart-shaped *millefiori* paperweight. The man cradled the glass heart in his palm like an egg plucked from its nest and offered it up for her examination. The "thousand flowers" caught the light and spoke a thousand words about love, romance, and beauty. I wondered if it was for Max, especially when she added in a silvery voice, "Wrap it, please. It's for someone special." I waited by the metal display rack until, package in hand, Max's mysterious friend glided out the door. Then I paid for the cards and backtracked to the café to find a table.

Daniela came along, settled Zola in a chair between us, and we placed our orders. Glancing at my cards, she said, "Cornell packages dreams. You do that too, with your writing." I felt Zola's warm breath on my arm as the waiter served us sandwiches made with an air-cured beef rubbed with rosemary and thyme.

Daniela dug into her bag for doggie treats. "Before Peggy bought this place, the Marchesa Casati lived here, strolling the gardens with cheetahs on diamond-studded leashes, spraying her houseboys gold, wearing snakes as necklaces. She was always famished for fresh audiences."

"You make her sound like a vampire," I said.

Daniela smiled. "In fact, some called her 'The Venus of Père Lachaise.'" When I pushed my plate aside at the mention of the cemetery, Zola's tongue made a swipe for the remains of my sandwich. "She loved attending costume balls and one time decided to disguise herself as Saint Sebastian. Her armor was pierced with hundreds of arrows that were supposed to light up, but when the marchesa was plugged in, her costume short circuited and the shock threw her flying into a backward somersault."

"Good grief. Did she survive?"

"She did. From then on she became obsessed with immortality and commissioned so many artists and sculptors that she managed to be portrayed more than any other woman, ever."

"More than the Virgin Mary?" I said.

"Ah, but she's a whole different story."

"I'm researching some of the Madonna paintings."

"Really? The local attitude toward Mary is interesting—devout, and at the same time, familiar. If *she* is your focus, then you must visit the Accademia to see Bellini's Madonna. It's quite breathtaking."

Daniela offered Zola a final bit of beef before attaching a bejeweled red leash to her collar. And forgetting about Cornell's tulle, feathers, and seashells, I cast a grateful smile at the elegant publisher and her terrier as we left the *Nonfinito*. I was living in Venice now, wasn't I, and my thoughts turned to the idea of transformation. A broken candy dish, a chance meeting at sunrise. I felt myself awaken when Daniela looped her arm through mine and we laughed together as the terrier, tail held high, led the way to the Accademia Gallery. In the distance, a voice was calling from the bank of the canal, "*La luce!*"

6

La luce non si riconosce se non attraverso l'oscurità.
There is no light without darkness.

A man with pomaded hair was pretending to add final touches to a canvas propped on an easel as he called again, "*La luce!*"

Daniela, noting his accent, whispered, "He's from Naples, luring tourists with work by novices at the art school, and pretending it's his own."

"*La luce!* The light!"

His shouting stirred Zola into a brief barking frenzy until Daniela scolded, "*Calma ti.*" Glancing over her shoulder, she said, "You know, Neapolitans and Venetians are said to be similar in that they talk with their hands and their women are closed, like clams." She pressed her palms together.

"I'm not so sure about the 'closed' part," I said. Thoughts of the blonde in the museum shop with the smug expression that suggested she was accustomed to having whatever she liked were interrupted when a man in a shabby suit, his gray hair in disarray, bumped into me.

I caught at his sleeve and received a blank stare from heavy-lidded eyes. "It's me—Claire," I said, hoping to nudge Gianni's memory. He appeared beyond disheveled, his face unshaven and his breath smelling sour. "We're supposed . . . "

"*Ah, si, si,*" he answered, and before I could make introductions, he brushed me off with, "The Madonnas, but just now I'm late for a meeting. *Devo scappere.* I must run." Ignoring Zola's low growl and Daniela's frown, he pushed by us, prompting Daniela to remark, "A peculiar fellow."

"He did seem a bit out of it."

At a kiosk near the museum's entrance, two men in cardigans hunched over a chessboard while a tiger cat slept on stacked copies of the daily paper. Partly obscured was a headline about the Iraq war and, just beneath, some mention of an art theft. When the cat rose and arched its back, Daniela scooped the terrier up and placed her in the tote. We entered the foyer of the museum, helped ourselves to brochures at the plywood reception desk, and pushed through the subway-like turnstile.

Note to Myself: The Accademia could consider upgrading its amenities.

The faint aroma of linseed oil and turpentine drifted in the gallery where a copyist worked on a duplication of Giorgione's *Tempest*.

"Venetian masters worked directly on the canvas," she was telling a visitor. "So their paintings have layers of under-drawings."

In the *Tempest*, a man stood on a riverbank gazing across the water at a nude woman who nursed her infant. A tenuous bridge stretched in the distance. But the man, the woman, and the bridge were all incidental to the bolt of lightning that marked the ominous sky. The woman stared straight out of the canvas. I felt the hairs rise on the back of my neck as her eyes bored into mine. She seemed to be saying, "*You* could be the one sitting on this riverbank."

Her stare and the feeling it stirred lingered with me as we moved on to Giovanni Bellini's paintings made creamy with layer upon layer of vegetable oil. Soft light touched the pearls strung through Saint Catherine's hair, continued across the Madonna's cheek, and fell on her little boy's innocent face.

"*She* knows how to hold a baby," I said, admiring Mary's strong, protective hands.

"Speaking of babies, this one needs to go outside," Daniela said, in response to Zola's whining. "We'll be right back."

As Daniela made her exit, the exotic couple from the Guggenheim entered the gallery and, taking no notice of me or anyone else, proceeded to Bellini's *Madonna degli Alberetti*, Our Lady with the Little Trees.

"Her shadow spills across the curtain," the man remarked, and then touching his nose to his companion's, whispered, "*Ti amo.*" He kissed the top of her head before turning back to the painting where his eyes lingered on the glimmer of distant hills. Then he sighed and slumped a bit.

The woman's face filled with alarm when the man took a step backward as if to steady himself. When his knees crumpled and his shoulder slid onto the marble floor, she scrambled over his supine figure, yanking at the red scarf and loosening his collar.

I jumped to my feet and shouted to the guard, "An ambulance, *per favore!*"

Cradling the man's head in her lap, the woman cried, "Stefan!" He looked like a feverish child with his cheeks flushed, his hands trembling. His eyes fluttered, and drenched in sweat, he whispered something that sounded like, "Overcome."

"Stendhal's Syndrome," I mumbled.

"What?" the woman said, staring up at me with her coal black eyes.

"No, nothing." This was no time to tell her about Stendhal, the French novelist who once entered a fugue state after overdosing on Renaissance art. Stendhal believed that art sometimes took on a life of its own and communicated with the afflicted. It was possible that Stefan would end up spending quality time with the *Virgin Flanked by Two Trees*.

Daniela came back as the medics were taking the stricken man's pulse, checking his eyes, and lifting him on a stretcher. The woman hovered close beside them as they left the room.

"What's going on?" Daniela said.

"One minute they were admiring a painting, and the next, he fainted."

I retrieved the cashmere scarf that had fallen to the floor unnoticed and stuffed it into my bag, saying, "I'm not leaving *this* at a plywood desk."

We continued to explore the city together, passing a workshop where a painting propped on an easel featured a convex mirror like those being sold inside. Its reflection revealed the entire fifteenth-century room: oranges glowing on a wooden chest beneath the window, a little dog at the bride's feet, even a reflection of the artist himself. Everywhere we turned there was a reminder that we were walking, talking, and breathing in a medieval village.

"During Carnevale, party-goers wore these and lost all inhibitions," Daniela said when we stopped at a shop of handmade masks.

"A sexual free-for-all, wasn't it?" I said.

"With immunity from consequence."

This would be right up Josie's alley. I remembered the story she told about smearing a blind date's body with Nutella. Those were the days when she was deep into Dante and rattling off lines like, *Nel mezzo del cammin . . .* She'd clutch at her breast and wave her copy of *Inferno* at me, proclaiming "*Hell* of a good read." Then, slapping the book shut, she'd tie back her wild, flaming hair, apply fresh lipstick, and boast, "Working on Circle Two, lasciviousness." These days, she claims to reserve the hazelnut chocolate spread for her surprise cupcakes.

"The *neutra*," Daniela was saying, "a blend of man and woman. And that one"—she indicated a pretty mask that resembled a cat's face—"the *gnaga*, a mask that gays wear to call to one another." I could just imagine Bernie and his French friend meowing at each other.

"Don't you think we all wear masks to some degree?" Daniela said.

"I know I do," I said, remembering a line that Josie loved to recite when she wasn't quoting Dante. *My profession is to be free.* George Sand had proclaimed this to the world as she darted from lover to lover. At the Père Lachaise, as I had watched a sparrow that flitted from Chopin's weeping muse to the corner post of a wrought-iron fence, I was reminded how Sand had flitted from Musset to Chopin, nursing him as he wrote his polonaises.

"As a travel writer, anyway. I'm a slave to my agent and end up writing formulaic entries about posh hotels and trodden paths. Something's missing."

"The element of surprise," Daniela said.

"That's for sure," I said. George Sand continued to write her novels while she cared for the composer. After his death, a hankie embroidered with her initials was found among the pages of his diary, along with a lock of her dark brown hair. I touched my own chestnut-colored hair. Who would want it?

Included among the festive assortment of sequins and feathers was the somber veiled *moretta*, a black velvet mask that had to be held in place by biting an attached button and beside it, a chalky mask with a prominent beak.

"Designed to hold herbs that protected the plague doctor," Daniela said. "Venice lost Giorgione and Titian to the plague, along with a third of her population. Recently a corpse was dug up with a brick jammed in her mouth because she had been suspected of spreading the disease as a vampire. Of course, the rats continued to arrive on ships and the doctor continued to give infected fleas a ride on his long coat."

I was tired of holding my feelings in, my white-hot anger and my profound grief. I was tired of wearing a mask, of biting a button, of swallowing a brick. And in the end I wasn't really protecting myself from those around me. I was protecting myself from *my self*. If I were to rip off the mask of perfection, would there be an underlying mask of the victim? And if I pulled that mask off, too, what would remain? I thought of Max and understood that one reason I found him so irresistible was that he wasn't overly concerned with being socially acceptable. He didn't care that his collar was frayed, that his Italian was poor, that picnics weren't allowed, that he had jam on his lip, that he might drop his cup. He wasn't afraid.

At the Bridge of Fists, Daniela and I bought apples from a greengrocer's boat moored by the walkway. Two pairs of white marble footprints on the bridge marked the starting position for fistfights. "With no rails," she said, "losers ended up in the canal." We had reached the high point, and the thought of falling brought a familiar queasiness that began to build, but the sickening feeling in the pit of my stomach disappeared when, released briefly from her tote, Zola danced around in delight to signal the arrival of Nicole and Etienne, the mother and son I'd encountered at the Boscolo pastry shop.

The two women greeted one another with kisses on each cheek, and Daniela explained, "Nicole and her husband, Pierre Lochon, attended one of my book events." Etienne came running up, waved to me, and stooped to throw his arms around Zola's neck.

"Oh, her publications are *délicieux*," Nicole was saying to me. "Food, love . . . and the spirit one brings to both. And always, always a bit of the unexpected, like dark chocolate in leek soup."

"Did I hear someone mention chocolate?" a familiar voice joined in. Shifting a large shopping bag, Josie came up behind me and gave my braid a tug. We had only been apart for a day, but I was glad to see her, and dying to tell her all about Max. That would have to wait, though. I made introductions.

"How is Pierre's research going?" Daniela said.

"Oh, he's obsessed with learning Chinese characters, thousands of them."

"Formidable," I said.

"He's using a memory palace to help him remember," Nicole said, rolling her eyes.

"Sounds poetic," Josie said. "But what is it?"

"He builds a palace in his mind and stores images he wants to memorize in the rooms. When he needs them, he imagines moving from room to room to collect them."

"Like memory coat hooks," said Daniela.

I pictured the Waverly paper covering the walls of my kitchen nook in Newburyport and Bernie's framed urban photos. An oak table from a New Hampshire antique shop, and two ladder-back chairs that my mother had cushioned in black and white toile, scenes of a couple picnicking by a lake. That's when I realized I had no desire to return to Newburyport. I didn't want to be reminded of my life there with Bernie.

The Russian in the museum may have fallen victim to Stendhal's Syndrome, but I could feel the entire atmosphere of Venice—sky, water, and palaces— pulling me into a painting that changed on the slightest whim, as if the artist were still adding a brush stroke here, another there.

"There's no cure for Polo fever," Daniela said in a clear voice that pulled me back to our small gathering on the bridge.

I wanted a picture of them, I told the three women, so they stopped talking long enough to pose for me. Daniela, her smooth hair glowing in the sunlight; Josie, flaming tresses contrasting with her green plaid forties outfit; and Nicole, soft curves and bulging tummy draped in supple gray jersey. Then I took a candid shot of Etienne and Zola playing together.

"Speaking of palaces," Josie said, "I've got to get home. This morning, I moved Boccaccio's cage and he threw a tantrum, so *my* palace is in a state of fucked-up feng shui."

Nicole giggled and called to Etienne, who, caught off guard, received a sloppy kiss from Zola. We stood there laughing at the tableau of the boy and the dog on the bridge without rails when a group of pedestrians approached. Among them, Max's unmistakable dark curly head bobbed above the blonde in her Versace dress, hanging on his arm.

"I have to be going, too," I said, feeling as if we were all in Cornell's world, the one where the needle of each compass points in a different direction. "I'll call you," I said to a retreating Josie.

"And, Claire, I'm staying at the Favretto," Daniela said.

"Perfect! I've booked a room there for Thursday. Goodbye Nicole, Etienne." As we parted, I glanced over my shoulder to see the terrier looking back at me, wagging her tail.

Venice boasts four hundred bridges: one of wood, one to sigh, one to struggle . . . three hundred and ninety-seven to go. I hurried around the corner and down several alleys before catching sight of Max and his companion far ahead, crossing the large, sunny Campo Santa Margherita. Keeping my distance, I followed them until they crossed the Ponte de Scalzi and continued along to the Ponte di Guglie. I trailed them up the dark alley that led to the Old Ghetto and finally to the doorstep of the synagogue where Max stopped to fish in his pocket for an oversized key.

Surprise Cupcakes

9 tablespoons unsweetened cocoa powder

1 1/2 cups flour

1/2 teaspoon salt

1 teaspoon baking soda

1/4 teaspoon baking powder

4 ounces unsalted butter, softened

1 1/2 cups granulated sugar

2 large eggs

1/2 cup hazelnut liqueur

1/2 cup milk

Jar of Nutella

Preheat oven to 350 degrees F.

Mix all dry ingredients in a bowl.

In a separate bowl, mix the milk and liqueur, and set aside.

In a separate mixing bowl, beat the sugar and softened butter together, mixing in one egg at a time until well blended.

Add the dry ingredients alternating with the milk mixture and mix well.

Pour into lined cupcake pans, 3/4 full. Bake for 20 minutes, and test with a toothpick. When the cupcakes have cooled, cut off the tops and slather them with Nutella. Cut a small circle in each cupcake using a sharp knife and fill with Nutella. Place tops on cupcakes and sprinkle with powdered sugar.

You'll think of something to do with the remaining Nutella!

7

Quando una freccia è incoccato sull'arco, prima or poi bisogna scoccaria.
When an arrow is poised on the bow, sooner or later it must fly.

Feeling let down, I retraced my footsteps, making my way to the Grand Canal where, at the waterside, the sun dropped between the rooftops like a coin in a slot, another day spent. I was no longer able to ignore the gnawing in my heart and in my stomach. One of these would have to be satisfied. I went searching for a plate of pasta and found on Calle Frezzeria—the Place of Arrow Makers—a restaurant with a self-service line. I carried my plate of steaming lasagna outside and claimed a table as tourists brushed by, following the same path that citizens in medieval times had taken to purchase their arrows.

There's a proverb that says, "Like the sped arrow, a lost opportunity does not return." Across the alley, a sleek, black arrow on the sign that read "per San Marco" brought back memories of Max. Feelings of vulnerability, recklessness, and desire made me quiver, and I wondered if I had lost whatever chance I might have had with him. I dug into my lasagna before it cooled and rated it as: excellent coming from a nondescript trattoria on a side street.

Window displays of the latest fashions caught my attention as I meandered back to the hotel. Dolce e Gabbana featured an uninterrupted reel of *The Seven Year Itch* playing on a suspended screen, its picture fuzzier than a mohair sweater. Nearby, Gucci showcased an elusive watercolor of wools in whispery pastel, along with fur bags barely large enough to hold lipstick and a few Euros. I was tempted to rethink my travel uniform: black pants, white shirt, and a black and white scarf. I wondered if the woman in the short story who tried to steal the chair looked anything like me. Maybe one day soon I'd venture into multicolored.

But for now, I collected my things at the Accademia and checked out. My routine while visiting a city is to stay at three or four different hotels. On the way to La Calcina, at the southeastern tip of Dorsoduro, I stopped to peek through openings in stone walls that hid gardens where the last of the persimmons clung to bare branches. I felt like one of those fleshy fruits, hanging on when the season's come to an end.

It was at La Calcina that John Ruskin wrote his masterpiece on Venetian art and architecture admired for its rich, rolling prose: *And the length of his sentence is like that of a long arrow that he draws to his ear and shoots light as a bird, straight as a bullet.* Crossing a small bridge, I entered the rose-colored building where the critic and his wife stayed in 1877.

At the desk, the darkly handsome concierge handed me an envelope and announced that a flood was predicted the following day. "*Si, acqua alta.*" He stared at my leather pumps. "In the cloakroom we have *Vellingtons* available to guests."

Wellingtons: thigh-high, green, and rubbery.

"*Va bene,*" I said, settling into an overstuffed love seat to read the note. My agent never failed to find me when a deadline loomed. But I lost concentration when a pair of knife-creased pant legs appeared within my line of sight. My eyes traveled up the legs to slim hips, broad shoulders in a fitted suit jacket, and . . . My gulp may have been audible. The striking man from the landing-dock introduced himself.

"Excuse me, I'm Michael, in town for the week." We shook hands and, before I knew what was going on, he sat down beside me and described his consulting work for Benetton, his historic house in Atlanta, and his silver Alfa Romeo. There was a spot of red on his collar where he'd cut himself shaving, and the dose of citric cologne was over-generous, as if splashed on in a hurry. *You're trying too hard,* I wanted to tell him. Another part of me wanted to give him a hug.

"We waited together for the waterbus," I said.

He cocked his head and studied me with his wide blue-gray eyes, perplexed.

"Pink mustache?" It wasn't registering, I could tell. He must have looked right through me out there on the landing dock, his smile not meant for me at all.

"I heard someone at the desk call you 'Claire.'"

"Ye-es?"

"Beautiful name, that's all. Reminds me of that piano piece, *Claire de Lune*." I returned my agent's letter to its envelope. "I see you're just settling in," he said, gesturing to my bag. "Will you join me for breakfast here tomorrow?"

"I'd be delighted." Even more delighted if it were Max, but I wasn't being fair to this kind-looking man.

"In the dining room, nine o'clock?"

I called Josie. She and Ethan had been out shopping for art supplies so that Ethan could work on some watercolors. "And what about *you*? It sounds as if you've had a full day."

"Ending with an invitation to breakfast tomorrow here at the hotel."

"Now *that* sounds promising."

That night from my balcony, I admired Ruskin's view of the pretty Zattere promenade, the broad canal, and beyond that, the island of Giudecca that stretched like a platter beneath the bulk of Venice's fish-shaped body. When reading Dante, Ruskin had been astonished that before Chiron spoke, Dante had the centaur divide his beard with the feathered end of an arrow. In Ruskin's collection of scattered letters, he claimed that Dante could not have imagined that gesture unless he had *actually seen it* in his poetic mind.

Satisfied that I was in good company in terms of "seeing things," I slipped between turned-down sheets that smelled as if they were just gathered from the line. I imagined Ruskin's reflection in the rococo mirror, Effie's hairbrush on the Chinoiserie bureau, and in the polished mahogany armoire, their clothes hanging side by side, not quite touching. I grieved for the incalculable space between them—the filmy dress, the dark jacket—then closed my eyes to stop my brimming tears.

My body stiffened when I heard a creaking sound, and I opened my eyes to discover a shade at the foot of my bed. Fiftyish, with large eyes, one lid drooping a little as if from fatigue, a white beard, and a thick head of white hair, combed to the side. From his buttoned brocade vest hung the gold chain of a pocket watch. Ruskin had once referred to Venice as a "splendor of miscellaneous spirits," and now he was one of them. Steadfast, he gave the impression of a stuffy conductor of the deep, steering me along the river of life.

"One must seek the truth in all things," he said in an authoritative tone.

"Which rules out composing landscapes in the studio," I said, offering my summary of his philosophy.

"It goes beyond that. Beware of *all* false beginnings." He went to the window, looked out at the Zattere and the night sky. "That's *my* view," he said. Then he floated out the window.

Zeno argues that an arrow can never reach its target because it has first to traverse the infinity of points between bow and target. A paradox, but in my meeting Max, it was as though Cupid had spotted me, shot from his bow, and definitely reached his mark.

"Beware of false beginnings," Ruskin had cautioned me. And my thoughts went springing from a bow, like arrows in search of truth. I fell asleep wondering where they would land.

8

Va sempre dritto!
Straight ahead!

As Michael and I carried our plates of fresh fruit and croissants to a table by the window, I noted that since my last review, the breakfast buffet was more popular than ever.

"This is my first time in Venice. Fall's best, isn't it?" he said, pulling a Street-Wise map from his pocket. "Not so crowded."

"Maps . . . " My mouth tingled with honeydew soaked in Asti. "They don't always work here. Sometimes you've just got to break down and ask directions."

"Yeah, and what you get is—*sempre dritto*." He rolled his eyes.

"Funny," I said, "but you *can* do that, keep going straight." He shook his head. "It's true. Considering the size of Venice, if you go straight ahead, you'll eventually get wherever you want."

"When I was a kid," he said, opening his map, "all my favorite books had maps: Hundred Acre Wood, Middle Earth. If there wasn't a map, I'd draw one. I'd be lost at the Benetton complex in Castrette without a map." I could see there was no sense repeating a favorite line of mine, that in Venice, your destination will find you.

"All right then," I told him, "let me show you the easiest way to get around. Picture Venice as a fish, its tail in the east . . . " I sketched the beginnings of a fish on a paper napkin. "And its lips in the west." I made them puffy, and puckered them up for fun. "The head in the north and the belly in the south.

Here you have the six *sestieri*." I divided the fish, marking the sections.

"So, right now we're . . . "

"In the fins." My pen rested on the location of La Calcina. "And you can get from the brains to the tail in no time at all."

"Okay, thanks," he said, flashing me a smile as he slipped the map into his jacket pocket and gave it a pat. The twinkle in his eye suggested that a playful nature lay beneath the stylish surface.

"What else do you do in Atlanta?"

"Mostly I'm busy as a consultant." He stared intently into my eyes. "And you're . . . divorced?"

I studied the backs of my hands, the pale indentation at the base of my ring finger. "Separated."

"You just never imagine it'll happen to you."

I stared at him, wondering how he could possibly know about Bernie. "Meaning?"

"At least, that's the way it was for me," he said. "One minute I was happily married—the next, she took off with my best friend."

"Oh. I'm sorry," I said, sipping my coffee.

"'What does he have that I don't?' I asked her. Know what she said?" Michael stabbed a melon ball with his fork. "'Let's just say he unites my colors.' That's what she said to me. Can you believe it?"

"That *is* pretty bitchy."

"I still don't know what went wrong. She got everything she ever wanted."

"Apparently not," slipped out before I could censor myself.

He blinked. "So what do you enjoy other than your writing?"

"Art, movies, travel, food." Like the Four Word Film Review, committed to summarizing the plot of a movie with abbreviated phrases such as Little Brains Face Fears for *Defending Your Life*, or Love's Arrow Rick-ochets Away for *Casablanca*, I could reduce myself to four words, as if my life were a film. Fag Abandons Adult Orphan.

"Me, too. Love them all. Plus fashion, of course." He checked his Rolex. "Sorry, I've got to meet some people at the plant. When can we get together again—soon, I hope?"

We exchanged business cards, and after Michael left, I lingered over my coffee, took hand lotion from my bag and squeezed some into my palm. Massaging my hands and the pale groove around my bare ring finger, I wondered if maybe one day someone would net a fish, cut it open, and discover my discarded wedding band. This had happened once with a doge's ring thrown into the water as a token of Venice's ceremonial wedding to the sea.

Strolling, I bumped into two Senegalese traders on the steps of the Rialto Bridge. They wore thin shirts that hinted of waving palms and drives across the savannah in an open Land Rover. Instead, they were struggling here in Venice, pushing phony designer bags from a blanket they could gather up in a hurry if the police arrived. Their lips had turned blue in the November morning, and they were hugging themselves. What would Saint Martin do? I wondered. Buying a knockoff Louis Vuitton wasn't an option, so I dashed off to the nearest clothing store and returned with a couple of thick wool turtlenecks. The two men let me photograph them, arms thrown around each other's shoulders, flashing the widest smiles of perfect, white teeth.

I said goodbye and drifted away from the water, trailing some boisterous students and ending up in the Campo Santa Margherita. At a neighborhood bar, two women in dark sweaters and sensible shoes sat at a small table, shopping carts parked beside them. One tossed down her espresso like whiskey, then confided to the other in Venetian dialect, "*El me piaxe, e no'l me piaxe.*" He pleases me, yet he doesn't please me.

I thought of Max—young, uninhibited—just starting his career, and imagined the inevitable misunderstandings, the operating at cross-purposes, the conflict that could sink us if we were a couple. Not to mention the beautiful woman forever at his side. Still, *el me piaxe*.

Then there was Michael, handsome, smart, level headed, close to my age. He reminded me of me—practical, cautious. The downside was that if we had too much in common, I could offer him no surprises and so would be unable to surprise myself.

When I was in fourth grade, my mother let me paper the family bathroom with National Geographic inserts that traced Marco Polo's three and a half year trek. All along the way, spirits beckoned him, Polo said, to abandon the path and walk into the desert, to become lost and die of thirst. At nine years old, such things concerned me. Do we stick to our predictable paths, or do we dare to wander off, take risks, and chance the unexpected? I worried about beckoning spirits and how to distinguish them from my own hopes and dreams.

During Polo's stay at Kublai Khan's court, more than a thousand cartloads of silk entered the capital every day, he said. But when he returned to his hometown, precious jewels sewn in the seams of his clothes, no one could believe the stories he told. Long voyages, great lies, they said, and they called him *Marco Il Milione*, for his million stories about the East.

I finished my coffee, and sparked by nostalgia for my early fascination with the Silk Road, I left the bar to search out Marco Polo's childhood home near the Rialto Bridge. When I reached the entry to the humble courtyard, I heard footsteps behind me and turned to discover a couple studying a map, the woman's brows knitted. A glimmer of recognition swept across her companion's face.

"From the museum," I said. "Claire." I rummaged through my bag and, as if performing a magic trick, pulled out the red scarf. "I knew we'd cross paths again."

"Very kind of you," Stefan said, returning my smile.

"Yuan-Ling," the woman said. She did not extend her hand, but folded the map and put it in her purse.

"Nice to meet you," I said.

"Nothing to mark the spot where the greatest traveler of all time was born. No statue. My grandfather spent years defending Marco against critics who claimed he never set foot in our country." Her black eyes held mine. "To be famous, they'll stop at nothing, even if it means stepping on Marco Polo's dead body!"

I knew an agenda when I heard one, and although I was no ambassador for Italo-Chinese relations, I made an attempt. "They *have* named the airport after him."

"Not good enough," she replied.

"And take a look at these," I said, pointing out images of flora and fauna carved in the thirteenth-century arch. Yuan-Ling shrugged and turned away. Only when Stefan draped his scarf around the branch of a nearby olive tree and arranged it in a bow, did her face soften. I took a picture of them there, his arm around her stiff shoulders. Behind them, the blur of a dilapidated building stood in the spot where, in the year 1295, Maffeo, Nicolò, and Marco Polo returned home after more than twenty years, unrecognized.

The three of us walked together to a closet of a bar where Stefan ordered a round of Aperol spritzers. Glancing at the life-size picture on the wall of Saint Lucia carrying her eyeballs on a platter, I skipped the olive.

"Sunset in a glass," Stefan said, toasting to our health as we stood at the counter.

The bartender brought us a plate of *cichetti*, open sandwiches no larger than silver dollars that someone had managed, perhaps using tweezers, to decorate with bits of artichoke, sprigs of asparagus and flecks of fish.

"So what brings you to Venice?" Stefan said.

"I'm a travel writer."

"And Yuan-Ling is a travel *guide*," Stefan said, "leading tours along the eastern sector of the Silk Road."

"Twenty days to Xi'an," Yuan-Ling said, her face no longer frozen.

Once the greatest city in the world. "What route do you take?"

"We skirt the southern edge of the Taklamakan Desert, stopping at Buddhist temples and ruins along the way."

"Well, I'm ready to sign up," I said to Stefan. "What about you?"

"Not just yet," he said. "But for our honeymoon, yes." He reached for Yuan-Ling's hand.

"It's all so magnificent," his fiancée said, "the trading post at Kashgar, the Loulan Beauty . . . "

I nodded, remembering a summer day at the Boston Public Library's long table, the antique wood cool under my arms. I was reading about the Beauty, named for her fine features framed by flaxen hair, and how she was buried four thousand years ago at the east end of the Taklamakan. How she was one of the blue-eyed people in tartans and leather shoes that not only built the now deserted Silk Road cities, but also brought Buddhism, horses, and saddles to China. But when I reached the passage describing the excavated bodies so perfectly preserved by the desert sand that traces of tears were found on the face of a mummified infant, I had hidden my face in folded arms and sobbed soundlessly—until my own tears stained the page.

"Yuan-Ling helped locate a pair of mummies in '96. A man carrying a bow and arrows," Stefan said, "and the woman, a mirror and comb."

"Also, an astronomy text," Yuan-Ling added, popping a sandwich suitable for a doll's tea party into her mouth.

"Just think, from the days of Confucius," I said. "Will you see the terracotta warriors?"

"Of course. We'll be there for four nights," Stefan said, a new note of pleasure in his voice. The anticipation of the evenings with his new bride excited him.

"You may know Pierre Lochon," I said. "He does research at the National Library."

"Registered for my spring tour," Yuan-Ling said, granting me a smile at last. I thought of Nicole with her bulging belly, and wondered how she would feel when her husband left her at home to care for a newborn and Etienne.

9

Niente si asciuga così presto come le lacrime.
Nothing dries faster than tears.

That evening I was lured to Saint Mark's Square by melodies that drifted from the café orchestras. Beneath the starry sky, couples clustered around flickering candles at the outdoor tables. A waiter in a white jacket lit someone's cigarette. Then a violin struck up the popular *"Con Te Partiro,"* and when the music reached the part where Bocelli sings about sailing a sea that no longer exists, a powerful longing settled in the deepest alcove of my being. The hunger ripped at my heart until I became the short-circuited Marchesa Casati, thrown for a loop. Anxious to escape the music and the feelings that surfaced, I rushed off in the direction of the Canal, tears throwing a veil over my path. Passing between the two columns of the *piazzetta*, I bumped into someone hurrying toward me.

"Oh, sorry," I said, pulling a tissue from my bag. My heart scampered when I realized it was Max.

"You okay?"

"This strong breeze . . . " I leaned against a column to steady myself. Dabbing at my eyes, I hoped that my mascara was waterproof.

Max glanced up at the statues of Saint Theodore and the winged lion of Saint Mark. "Is this where they dangled the prisoners in cages?"

I shuddered, giving my nose one last pinch with the tissue. "The fatal pillars, known for bad luck."

"Good luck tonight, though, running into you. Are you busy?"

"I was about to take a waterbus out to the lagoon," I said, feeling a rush of warmth. Good luck?

He shifted his books from one arm to the other. "Mind if I come along?"

"That would be nice," I said, trying not to act too eager. My heart was galloping as we boarded and even as the boat carried us toward a spit of sand stretching like an arm that protected Venice from the Adriatic. I tried to slow my breathing to the rhythm of the boat's chugging. "You mentioned that you study art history."

"Just finished my doctorate at Harvard. Do you write while you're traveling?"

"Mostly take notes. I do most of my work and all my revisions at home, in Newburyport."

"Only an hour from Cambridge," he said. The dark shape of a huge ocean-going cruise ship loomed on the horizon, its portholes glowing like the pearls in Saint Catherine's hair. Somewhere a bell buoy clanged.

An easy drive, I wanted to tell him.

After dropping off the Lido passengers, our *vaporetto* turned back toward the city. Max and I talked about Cornell's constructions and the Madonna paintings, the spirit of Venice, the value of art. In the distance, we could see above each waiting station, a neon banner glowing in blue block letters. SHIPS PASSING IN THE NIGHT was the first to seep through the fog and into my subconscious. It flooded me with longing.

"My grandmother had a perfume bottle that same blue. I forget the name." Max said, leaning against the rail.

"Evening in Paris?" The fragrance guaranteed to deliver silver stars, stolen kisses, and dancing in the dark.

He nodded. "She escaped from Germany carrying it in her purse. To keep her dreams alive, she told us."

A gondola flitted past, its steel beak flashing. When I rubbed my arms to fend off the cold, Max draped his jacket around my shoulders. And when I leaned against him and he put his arm around me, I shivered not with the cold, but with a mixture of fear and desire.

We debarked at Riva Schiavoni and strolled beneath lamps that cast rosy pools of light on the waterfront promenade. I wanted to ask Max about the woman I saw him with, but I didn't dare. It had been so long since I spent time with any man other than Bernie, and it felt good, really good, to be with Max. It was so different than being with a detached Bernie. I liked the feel of Max's arm around me, the weight of his jacket, the woodsy smell of his sweater. We stopped to admire a display of glossy coffee-table books in one of the shops.

"Let's go in," I said, wishing there were private rooms with cushy beds, classical music, and fine art.

Max picked up a book about the island of Burano and flipped through photos of fishermen's houses, all brightly painted. "Straight from Matisse's palette," he said, and when he added, "Want to go, maybe this weekend?" I was filled with hope that we weren't ships passing in the night on life's ocean, distant voices in the darkness. We were making plans.

We found a corner table next door at Harry's Bar and ordered two Bellinis.

"This is the pink Bellini uses for the Madonna's cheek," I said, turning my flute of blended peach juice and Prosecco to catch the light. "And the color of her baby's lips and pudgy toes."

"Tastes like summer," Max said.

Nearby, a group of Americans in blazers ordered martinis and thin slices of raw beef called *Carpaccio*, in honor of that painter's deep red used for Joseph's robe. This room was Hemingway's hangout, and the woman in shredded jeans at the next table stirred a celery stalk in a Bloody Mary, Hemingway's poison.

"Cozy," Max said, surveying the room.

"That's the strange thing about Harry's. Feedback can run the gamut, from a soulless closet to minimalist chic. For me it's a place to slip into yourself—the self of your dreams."

"I feel myself slipping now," Max said, leaning sideways and pretending to fall off his chair. He reached across the table for my hand.

"Transportation strike tomorrow," the woman in jeans announced to her companion as she slid her backpack beneath the nearby table. "I'm gonna miss the boat rides, but we'll manage. I've got to do something about my heel, though. Look at it!" The blister was a huge, watery blob, a purply-red escaped from Carpaccio's palette.

I reached into my bag and, handing her a Band-aid, said, "Here you go."

"Thank you sooo much," she said. "You're a lifesaver!" She batted her eyes at Max, but her gesture was lost on him.

"I need to check my mail," he said once we left Harry's and headed toward the Cannaregio district. "Things have been hectic because of this lecture I'm giving Friday—in Italian."

"Really?" His delivery of a single phrase spoken in the piazza had been pretty rough. Now he planned to tackle entire paragraphs.

"At the Ateneo Veneto, eight o'clock." We walked past a window of hand-blown glass and another of gilded stationary. "Want to come?"

When I tucked my arm in his and he pressed it to his side, I felt as buoyant as the blonde must have felt with him. We walked that way until we reached Planet Internet with its sterile walls and fluorescent lights, and took our seats, side by side.

Max squinted at his monitor and said, "My Mom's sick. Don't think it's serious, though. You checking in with your folks?"

I had avoided the topic because there was never a right time to talk about the accident, the heartbreaking newspaper photos branded on my inner lids. But this was as good a time as any, and I recounted the horror in a flat voice, the only way I could get through the story without falling apart. Max leaned forward, put his hand on my elbow, held it firmly as if to usher me through the most difficult passages. Then we both sat quiet for the longest time.

"I'm sorry, Claire," he said. "Should we go?"

I nodded. "I'm feeling tired. Stay if you need to, but I'd better go back to my room." I reluctantly slid his jacket from my shoulders and handed it to him.

"And where's that?"

"La Calcina," I said.

"Where Ruskin stayed."

"I like to follow in the footsteps of the famous, see the same views they saw, from the same windows."

"Hmm. Ruskin's the grump that called the basilica a heap of sculptured sea foam." Max stood close, smelling of moss and murmuring pines. "Let's go for dinner after my talk, and I can fill you in on him." In the artificial light, his eyes were the color of chestnuts flecked with gold. "Will you meet me at the auditorium? A friend is helping me with my translations."

I pictured the woman in Versace and felt a strong dose of jealousy swirl in my chest. "Yes. I'd love to," I said.

Later, when Josie called my room, I told her all about my past few days.

"He's a bit eccentric," I said, describing Max.

"Always a plus."

"Kind of young, though, and I think he may be taken."

"I wouldn't be too sure. The point is, Claire, you need to let go and enjoy yourself and . . . . Oops, the doorbell." We said goodbye, and I smiled, thinking Boccaccio might be up to his old tricks.

In the morning, I wandered around Cannaregio, ending up in a neighborhood so quiet that I could hear a sneeze from across the canal. The Madonna dell'Orto was built here and dedicated to Our Lady when somebody found her statue buried in a nearby vegetable patch. It was here that Tintoretto was put to rest. Or not.

I no sooner stepped over the threshold than I detected a whiff of garlic along with the incense. Like a conscientious tour guide, the apparition of Jacopo Robusti Tintoretto appeared.

The great master waved his hands toward the church's bold paintings full of light and movement, his booming voice bouncing off the brick-faced interior. "*Sì*, more than forty-five feet high, the tallest Renaissance paintings on canvas. Some say this was all to challenge my rival, Veronese. But believe me this was never, what do you call it, a pissing contest. With Veronese or anyone else!" Tintoretto was so worked up, his beard quivered.

He pointed to the *Last Judgment* over the high altar. "Well, check it out! The world melted into limbs and bones, corpses and heaving clay. I was so pleased that Ruskin's wife, that meek little woman, ran from the church, screaming."

When I pulled out a stick of gum and chewed noisily, Tintoretto took off. It was time for me to ditch all these ghosts with their nerve-wracking agendas. I needed to catch the ear of an understanding woman, so I stepped into the chapel to consult with the *Madonna of the Vegetable Patch*.

"You were buried, then discovered" I touched her chalky blue robe. "Restored and brought to light."

The Madonna's face was as calm as unstirred waters, her expression as infinite as a cloudless sky. It may have been an illusion created by the flickering candles, but I perceived the faintest of empathetic nods. I lingered in the comfort and safety of the sacred space and inhaled the refreshing scent of celery, carrots, tomatoes.

Across the room a cat curled beneath an empty easel that had once held a *Madonna and Child* by Bellini, stolen in 1993 and yet to be recovered. I tried to imagine, squinting in that direction, the Madonna's deep red dress and dark cloak, her reproachful expression, and her young son, staring at his mother open mouthed, a hand on his chest, shocked that anyone would dare thrust them in harm's way.

As I stroked the waking cat, it stretched its legs, reaching toward me with its double paws, claws extended, its mouth opening in a yawn that revealed dainty white teeth. I left her there, blinking and purring, and continued to the Santa Maria dei Miracoli, a church that resembles a jewelry box and houses a miracle-working Madonna. As I entered, shafts of light streamed through the windows, creating a glow around the Virgin and Child at the altar. Kneeling on the cold stone, I whispered, "Please, just help me get over Bernie's betrayal." And I couldn't help but add, "That lying little creep." My clock was ticking, and what did I have to show for myself—a few dreams sandwiched between book covers. Would I be able to cross the forgiveness bridge when I came to it?

A resolute voice broke the quiet.

"You must crowd out your fears and your grief by filling your heart with love."

"My Lady?"

"Love will melt the snow of the most frozen regions. Take the plunge, swim in the waters."

If anyone had license to mix metaphors, it was the Madonna. Fill my heart with love, and swim. I lit a candle and left the church, planning to stop by Harry's. On my way, I passed the statue of a man in a cap and loose-sleeved gown, wearing a bronze nose guard, perhaps the price he paid for sticking that body part into other people's business. It was the tradition for those disappointed in love to stuff their sad little slips of paper up the statue's sleeve. *Sior Rioba* was the disenchanted lover's stand-in for the lion's mouth. There was no council to dispense justice for crimes of the heart, but here lovers were able to get their complaints off their chests. I didn't bother, though, because Mary had given me hope.

At Harry's, I took the same table Max and I had shared the night before and ordered the same drink. It was in this corner that my favorite travel writer, James Morris, hung out half a century earlier with Allied officers and members of the aristocracy. And it was here that he said he felt at one with all writers who did their work in corners of bars and coffee shops.

Harry's Bar was part mirror, part memory palace. The woman in jeans said such-and-such. A man and a woman at a table spoke of this and that. It was all about your expectations and how they played out. Max had talked of taste; I spoke of tints; and a young woman with a blister had worried about transportation. My eyes scanned the room, and my heart gathered up all the words, scents, and emotions of the night before.

Long shadows fell across the path I followed to the San Polo district, and as soon as I reached Ca' Favretto, I phoned Daniela to make plans for dining in the hotel's restaurant. After dressing for dinner, I threw open the window to gaze at the palaces across the water. They stood like a group of conspirators. *Di mai*, they seemed to call across the water, *di mai* . . . always . . . never.

"Wonderful view of the Canal," Daniela said, ordering her terrier to "*Stai brava!*" as Zola scrambled under the table, searching for a comfortable spot.

There would be no woeful spirits tonight with my friend seated opposite me and Zola draping herself over my feet. The waiter filled our water glasses and slid a bowl under the table for Zola, as the violin notes in Vivaldi's "Autumn" blended with the comforting sounds of clinking utensils and soft chatter.

Although I offer readers survival tips for solo dining, I personally hate eating alone. Go ahead, plunk yourself down at the bar and strike up a conversation, I encourage them, or scribble notes at the table and get mistaken for a food critic. Ask about a favorite dish and get invited into the kitchen. But one of the many reasons I love Venice is that you *can* dine alone, standing unnoticed at a bar or seated in the informality of a *trattoria*.

So this was a special treat for me, to share a table with a companion in the lovely restaurant of a hotel for dinner. When my new friend rattled off our order, ending with "*grissini,*" Zola's tail could be heard thumping at the mention of breadsticks wrapped in thin slices of spicy ham.

Daniela clasped her hands, diamonds sparkling. "A perfect view of the Ca' d'Oro," she said as we peered across the Grand Canal's ribbon of water. One of the oldest, the palace threw its reflection across the dark surface like a swath of fine lace. While Daniela reached under the table with a treat for Zola, my eyes strayed to the pink palazzo. The tall windows of the *piano nobile* offered a view of the room's interior where an ornate mirror caught the blazing light of a Murano chandelier and reflected several figures moving about. A regal blonde in a simple shift offered wine to two guests.

In an ancient diary, a man living in Venice described how his neighbors shared the "amiable custom" of studying one another's faces through opera glasses. One day, a woman stared at him from her large window across the canal. And when she was sure that she had caught his eye, she cast a glance back into her room, in the direction of her life-size mirror, inviting him to appraise her reflection.

But the guests in the pink palazzo were oblivious to my studying them from across the water, and no one was issuing an invitation.

"Are you enjoying your stay?" Daniela said.

"Very much." I felt Zola's tongue on my ankle. "So the books you publish. Nicole mentioned . . . "

"I have a passion for personal stories and recipes. That's why I like your work, the way you tie in historical anecdotes with places." I wondered what it would take to keep Zola licking my ankle. "And the proverbs, of course. They're like *cichetti*, those delectable little tidbits."

"One of my favorites is 'Either eat this soup or jump out the window.'" I waved my spoon for emphasis. "Even better with the Italian rhythm and rhyme—*O mangiar questa minestra . . .* "

" *. . . o saltar questa finestra,*" Daniela said, completing the phrase. "Certainly more lively than 'Take it or leave it.' So your visit, any new insights?" She drew the spoon from her bowl of duck soup and quietly sipped from its side, rolling her eyes heavenward.

"To tell the truth, I'm still reeling from a breakup with my husband."

"I see." Daniela, putting her spoon down, was poised to listen.

"I had quite a shock in Paris, where I left him."

"In Paris. I'm sorry to hear that," she said, her voice soft, a distant look on her face.

"Since I've been here, though, I've met a couple of interesting men."

She perked up, her eyes brightening. "And?"

"There's Michael, a businessman, kind, feet on the ground, and Max, a young professor of art history." I emphasized the word "young."

"And . . . " She a made gentle loop in the air with her soup spoon, urging me to go on.

"I'm not sure I trust either of them."

"Because of what happened between you and your husband? But tell me more about these two."

"Max is spontaneous, exudes a sense of wonderment, but he's several years younger."

"So much the better." Daniela's eyes twinkled. "*Cara*," she said in response to my weak smile, "a few years, that's nothing. Look at you, a true beauty. What difference . . . . There's something else, isn't there?"

"I've seen him with another woman."

"Ah, so there's intrigue, too. Americana?" She had lost all interest in the soup.

"No, I think she may live in the palace next to the Ca' d'Oro."

"The pink one? Why, that's the Massinis' palazzo—Professor Massini specializes in the history of film, and his wife, Isabella, is also an academic. That family has lived there for six hundred years. You worry too much." Zola licked my ankle again. "Your Max is in good company."

"But I've seen them together, and they look . . . involved."

"A flirtation, at most. The Jews of Venice simply don't do more than that. They've survived here for six centuries. And not by getting divorced!"

Maybe.

Zola jumped into my lap and licked my face.

"Sorry if she takes advantage. She's quite fond of you."

Daniela wanted to hear all about Max, and every detail from the coffee cup on his knee to the Florian chair to his deep, brown eyes flecked with gold took us through our main meal. When I finished, Daniela responded with, "*Un colpo di fulmine!* The thunderbolt. It often strikes when one is vulnerable." Her eyes changed expression as if recalling a thunderbolt of her own.

"But that's just it," I said. "I don't want to fall victim to . . . "

"No, no. Think of it another way, that you are open to change."

Over at the pink palace, a lone woman examined a display of miniatures on the far wall while a young man in a ponytail photographed a handsome curly-haired man in front of a large oil painting. The man turned from the painting to sit on a sofa, and although his back was toward me, I recognized the slope of his shoulder and his thick, black hair.

"He's at the palazzo right now," I said, leaning forward.

"How extraordinary." Daniela narrowed her eyes, giving the scene her full attention.

"When I left Bernie in Paris," I said, half to myself, "I felt like Laica, you know, the Soviet dog sent into outer space on Sputnik."

"Your life has been that tragic?"

"My husband cheated on me with a man named Eric."

Daniela shook her head. "*Miseria.*" Her mistress's shift in tone triggered a soft whimper from the terrier.

"I should have realized sooner that he was drawn to men, but I didn't want to. Everyone adored him." I glanced down. "Stray dogs lapped at his heels." Daniela patted my hand. "He cried along with me at all the romantic movies."

"That kind of tenderness can be so seductive."

"But just last month, I caught him . . . "

"Tsk, tsk," said Daniela.

The terrier poked her head out from under the tablecloth hoping for another morsel. Over at the pink palazzo, the crowd had thinned.

"You know, I haven't been in a gondola for some time. How about you?"

When I refrained from describing the disposal of Bernie's clothes, Daniela continued, "Franco, at the hotel pier, is an engaging fellow. Won't you join me?"

"That's sweet of you, but . . . " A shadow of disappointment swept across Daniela's face. Zola let out a soft whine.

"On second thought," I said, giving the dog a scratch behind the ear, "I'd love to."

The dark of night exposed all the interiors invisible by day—a couple playing cards, a cozy fire in a hearth, a cocktail party for academics. Glimpses of other worlds, like the beginning sequence in the movie *Possessed*, where Joan Crawford looks into the windows of a slow-moving train and the passengers inside represent everything she dreams of having in her own life.

As our gondola glided along the world's most memorable main street, Franco, balanced at the stern, became a cutout shape reciting some history of the glittering palaces and their inhabitants. He asked us to imagine Lord Byron swimming the canal in the middle of the night, holding a torch in one hand to alert sleepy gondoliers. He showed us where Robert Browning stayed, Titian's workshop, Desdemona's house, the palace where a string of owners died shortly after signing the purchase and sale, a façade decorated with glittering mosaics meant to advertise the Murano glassworks, palaces where Wagner composed and where Monet painted, the circular windows that interested Ruskin.

"Life reflects what we bring to it," he said as his long oar stirred scents of moss and musk that mingled with the salt air, "and Venice is like a jeweler's loupe. It magnifies everything."

"How true," Daniela said. "Now would you be kind enough to sing a *barcarola*, Franco?"

"I cannot refuse such a lovely lady," the gondolier said, giving a slight bow, and in a honeyed tenor, he sang:

Come with me, we shall get into a gondola and go forth on the sea.
Cooling breezes fan the air, inviting all to sleep without a care.

Zola snored at our feet while Daniela and I luxuriated in our velvet chairs. In bed later that night, I dreamed of a long, winding passenger train. I wasn't standing on the station platform; I was aboard the train, walking from car to car, searching the compartments for an empty seat, confident that there was one waiting for me.

Bellini
(created by Giuseppe Cipriani in 1943)

1/3 glass of white peach puree
2/3 glass chilled Prosecco

Slice fresh peeled peaches and blend in a food processor. Serve in tall champagne flutes.

To recreate the tint used by Giovanni Bellini for the Madonna's cheek, puree fresh raspberries in a food processor and add 3 drops to each glass.

10

Chi fa falla e chi non fa sfarfalla.
Those who act make mistakes;
those who do nothing flit around like lost butterflies.

We were enjoying breakfast together when Daniela asked about my family.

"Devastating," she said, when I explained what had happened. She gave a shudder, patted my hand, and told me how truly sorry she was. Then we both sat quiet for a long time, gazing out the window at the clear, blue sky. When she finally turned to me, her hazel eyes a swirl of the warm browns of continents and greenish blues of oceans, she held my gaze, a thoughtful expression on her face.

"You know, bad things happen to us all. And that was a terrible thing, to lose your parents that way. But Claire, what matters most now is the way in which we deal with these tragedies and the way we live out the rest of our days. It's a shame that our time together is so short. If it weren't for my appointment in Milan . . . "

"We'll meet up again," I said.

"Better than that, manage a trip together one of these days," Daniela said.

"Really? Where are we going?"

Daniela laughed. "Paris. I have contacts there."

"I'm not sure," I said, slumping in my chair. "I don't know if I'm ready to deal with Paris."

"You will be," she said, standing to give me a kiss on each cheek.

The scent of her Chanel hung in the air as I left to check my mail at Planet

Internet.

"Oh," I said in surprise, my eyes stinging, when a message popped up from Bernie. He'd discovered a way to get a quickie divorce for $250 online. All I had to do was complete the attached form and papers would be filed in court. His treat, he wrote. What a guy. And it would only take half an hour. I didn't have to let him call all the shots, I knew, but after what he pulled in Paris . . . it was better this way, almost breezy.

The form was straightforward and matter-of-fact: name, birthdate, birthplace, social security number, date and place of marriage.

A beautiful day in June, ten years ago, on my family's front lawn where I had somersaulted as a toddler, searched for four leaf clovers as a Scout, performed cartwheels as a teen, and tied the knot at thirty-five. Newburyport, Massachusetts.

I remembered the stargazer lilies, tulle on tabletops, the love letter openers, one for each guest.

Thirty minutes later, I hit the send button. As I was about to log out, a message appeared from Michael. "I miss you! Call me."

On the phone his voice held a boyish exuberance, an innocent sense of expectancy. "I've got the morning free. Want to go exploring?"

"What do you have in mind?" I said.

"The Rialto market and some place nice for lunch. How about if I meet you at your hotel in half an hour?"

At the Rialto, we passed a cluster of produce boats and stallholders and stopped to sniff the golden pears and rosy apples. A fishmonger lifted the gill of a sea bass to show that the blood was bright, while in the distance, another peddler sang, "*Caro nome che il mio cor . . .* " And our vendor replied with "*qual piùma al vento.*"

"Translate?" Michael said.

"Women are as fickle as a feather in the wind."

"Ah."

We moved along to bowls of glistening *botargo*, boxes of squirming eels, and pans of twitching shrimp.

"Can there be anything on earth more tempting than my prosciutto, salami, parmigiano?" a white-aproned vendor called, spreading his arms wide. We helped ourselves to samples of everything.

"I'd like to take this place home with me," Michael said.

"Do you cook?"

"I can fire up a grill."

"And drop things in boiling water?" I teased, recalling the lobster scene in *Annie Hall.*

"That, too."

We bought a bag of pistachios and lounged near a kiosk, shelling and eating them. Nearby, a woman with a cartful of wooden toys was manipulating a Pinocchio marionette.

"The boy who told everyone he was real," I said, "when he knew he wasn't." I could hear the anger in my voice. After all, I'd fallen victim to manipulation and lies.

"But he followed his instincts in tough situations, and in the end—you've got to hand it to the little guy—he finally got it right."

Humph.

That's when I told Michael why I had arrived in Venice earlier than planned and stayed with Josie.

"I'm sorry about all of that, Claire, but I'm awfully glad that you and I happened to be here at the same time. Otherwise, I never would have met you." A Madonna statue crowned with a halo of colored lights marked the little bar where we joined vendors in their large white aprons standing at the counter drinking a local wine that hinted of violets.

"In a way, you remind me of a violet," Michael said.

"Really?"

"You know, kind of shy, modest. Maybe even reclusive. Tucked away in a forest somewhere."

"I keep some things to myself, but *reclusive?* I'm out here with you, aren't I?"

"What I meant to say was *mysterious.*"

"Less so now that I've shared this disaster with you?"

"Still."

We explored some of the souvenir shops on the Rialto Bridge, joking about the glow-in-the-dark gondola toys and tacky masks, and ending up at Al Graspo de Ua for the luncheon buffet.

"Bunch of Grapes," I translated for Michael.

As we filled our plates and headed to our seats, dodging copper pots and ropes of garlic that hung from the rafters, I spotted Max and Isabella across the room seated with another couple, just finishing coffee. Max had his back to me. Isabella wore a half-smile, reminding me of Botticelli's *Venus on a Half Shell*. That's how beautiful and delicate she looked in her pearls and cashmere cardigan. She turned in my direction as if she could sense my eyes on her. Then she reached over and, with a smile, squeezed Max's arm and whispered something in his ear.

"*Chi ga' bon apetito . . .*" Michael was leaning back in his chair, struggling to read a handwritten proverb on the wooden beam above our heads. "*No ga' . . .*"

"One who has a good appetite has no need of sauce." I considered Michael from across the table and wondered if I would be willing to do without the sauce that Max promised.

Michael continued to tip backwards, trying to read the last few words aloud. And then, *bam*, he was on his back on the floor, a stunned expression on his face. In the time it took me to push my chair from the table, Max arrived.

"You okay?" he asked, helping Michael to his feet.

"I had the wind knocked out of me, but I'm fine," Michael said, brushing his pants and straightening his jacket while Max righted the chair. "Thanks." The two introduced themselves and shook hands.

"Nice to see you," Max said to me.

"You know each other?" Michael said.

"Oh, yes," Max said, smiling.

When Max returned to his table, I asked, "*Are* you okay, Michael?"

"No goose eggs," he said, rubbing the back of his head.

"Let's see." I stood beside him, ran my fingers through his hair. Gently exploring the terrain of his scalp, I murmured, "I'm so sorry about your fall."

"I'll be fine. It's just a little embarrassing. It was nice of your friend to come over. Do you know each other through work?"

"No, we met only recently, by chance."

"Seems like a nice guy."

After Michael and I parted with a brief kiss at the entrance to the Danieli, I treated myself to a soak in a tub of warm water littered with rose petals. Eyes closed, I fantasized about Musset and George Sand and the way they wore out their pens and their passion in this very room. "Love exists," George wrote. "It isn't an illusion. You only have to recognize it." After I dried off and applied lotion to my face and throat, I studied myself in the mirror and wondered if I were able to recognize love. And what about Daniela—could she detect the difference between what she called a harmless flirtation and a full-blown affair?

The walls and ceilings of the large assembly room were plastered with murals of *Purgatorio* and *Passione*, the prodigal son and good Samaritan, paintings that soared above the audience, dwarfing the local women in their knee-high rubber boots and the men sporting waders that reached to their thighs. I took a chair close to the podium, stretched my toes in my stylish mini zip-up boots, and began to feel a little foolish.

When the World War II siren sounded a flood warning, sobering everyone with its forlorn wail of sixteen blasts, I regretted not grabbing that pair of Wellingtons offered by the concierge. The chatter escalated. Everybody was wondering aloud how long to stay before seeking refuge in the second and third stories of their homes.

Isabella took the center stage to make introductions. A soft-spoken professor in thick glasses and tweed jacket offered further comments. Then Max adjusted the microphone and read in careful Italian about Venetian art in the Middle Ages as Isabella sat beside him, following along with her copy and silently mouthing the words. At the end of the lecture, Max wanted to show some slides. But just as the first image projected on the screen, a second series of alarms blared, more persistent this time. A flock of *anziani*, old ones, perched like blackbirds on the edge of their seats, gathered their belongings and fled. Isabella bid Max goodnight and left the stage, hurrying to meet a man about her age, perhaps her husband, who handed her a pair of high boots. The other professor delivered a brief thank you into the microphone and wished everyone a safe trip home. Then, appraising Max's loafers and my inadequate footwear, he warned, "No matter how high the water gets, do not remove your shoes. If you cut your feet, they will be infected." The place emptied in minutes.

"Great job with the Italian," I said.

"Thanks. I had a lot of help from Isabella." Max gathered his papers, unplugged the projector and slid it into its case. "Hungry?"

"Starving!"

"There's a *trattoria* near my apartment."

The floodwaters had already reached the Ateneo's top step. Dark, cold water pushed around the soles of our shoes then rose to our ankles as we descended the stairs, feeling for the pavement. Flooding waters raged with a force so great that Max grabbed my hand, pulling me along. Unable to figure out where the walkway ended and the canal began, we stayed close to the buildings, realizing that with one false step we'd be in the drink. A bridge without rails seemed like a walk in the park compared to finding our way in this *acqua alta*. When the water grew higher, reaching our knees, I stopped to roll up my pant legs, but it was useless.

"Better keep moving," said Max, a strain in his voice.

Abandoning all thoughts of keeping any part of us dry, we sloshed and pushed through the icy water, wading past temporary walkways stacked off to the side like picnic tables.

"They might have come in handy." Max squeezed my hand tighter.

High tide, low pressure, and north winds were working against us. As the water rose above our knees, we tried even harder to push ourselves onward while waiters were gathering tablecloths and others piling chairs in a restaurant built to resemble a ship's cabin. In the lobby of a posh hotel, thick Persian carpets were being rolled. Four men were stowing a grand piano. The owner of a tobacco shop struggled to sweep rushing water back over his sandbagged threshold.

"Can't he get out?" Max said.

"If he wants. All doors in Venice open inward," I said. The water had reached my thighs.

"Maybe we should wait for a *vaporetto*," Max said, glancing at a group of middle-aged American tourists who sat on the landing stage.

"I don't think they're running."

"Then let's try to get to my place on foot," Max shouted over the roar of the water.

"The entrance to the Old Ghetto is the first to flood," I told him, fear pushing my voice up an octave. "I was eating at the Israeli restaurant during a minor flood, and by the time I finished my couscous, the walkways around the Ghetto had disappeared."

Max wiped his face with his sleeve and held his projector higher. "Let's give it a shot, anyway." As we turned into the Ghetto's hidden entrance, water lapped at the restaurant's step.

"Fortunately the synagogues are on higher ground," Max said as we reached the door to his building and could once more see our shoes and the brickwork beneath them. He unlocked the carved door and swung it open to pitch black. In the musty stairwell, I tried the wall switch.

"Someone hasn't paid the electric bill," I said, my goofy statement reflecting my nervous anticipation.

"Disconnected for Shabbat." Max led me up the worn, marble stairs and opened the door to the apartment. Inside, he groped around for a chair and guided me to it. I yanked at my boots, wet inside and out.

"Here, let me help you." When his warm breath hit my knee, I nearly tipped over.

"Can't use the gas stove," he said, "with the rabbi next door. Are you still willing to try the *trattoria*?"

My boot came off with an embarrassing sucking sound. I could only imagine what mysterious sea creatures may have spilled out along with the water.

"If you think we can make it."

Max peeled off my socks and rubbed my feet until they grew warm. "I've got sneakers you can wear."

"Thanks," I said in the direction of the disembodied voice. "What about you?"

"I'll change into dry socks and cover them with plastic bags. Wear the same shoes. It's an old camping trick."

"About Shabbat. Do you follow these traditions at home, no lights?"

"Not really, but I like the *idea* of Shabbat, to create an island in time."

Max's sneakers felt big and clunky, like clown shoes, but they were dry and, I hoped, not red. The rest of me remained a soggy mess. We made our way down the stairs and emerged into the square where lamps glowed from behind the wine-colored drapes of the Levantine synagogue.

"They get to have lights," I said.

"Turned on before sundown and remaining on until after sunset tomorrow." We entered the hollow darkness of the New Ghetto where apartment buildings loomed around us, a reminder that the ghetto's inhabitants could only build up.

A bulky man lugging an accordion led us past a darkened storefront window where orthodox Jews in fedoras bowed in prayer. We followed him to the Rio di San Girolamo, spanned by a small humpbacked bridge that resembled an inchworm arching to move trustingly from leaf to outheld stick. As Max and I reached the high point of the bridge, the clouds parted to reveal a moon that had tripled in size.

We stopped and, looking up, he said in a teasing voice, "Do they get to have more stars here?"

"*Everything* is more in Venice. The light's more magical. The homes are grander, the artisans more gifted . . . "

"And the water is wetter."

Gazing at the sky, I'd lost all points of reference and felt as if I were falling into the heavens.

"In the spirit of Shabbat, I have a story for you," he said. "A short one," he added, when he heard my heavy sigh.

With his hand on my waist, we continued to study the stars. "Von mornink," Max began, assuming a heavy Yiddish accent, "long ago, the rabbi came upon one of his disciples rushing through the streets.

"'The sky, have you seen it this morning?' he asked the man.

"'No,' the man said.

"Then the rabbi asked, 'Have you seen the street this morning?'

"'Oh, yes,' the man said, 'the streets I have seen—the men and women coming and going, buying and selling.'

"Then the rabbi said . . . " Max's face was so close to mine his eyes looked as if they, too, had tripled in size. "'In one hundred years, everything in the streets will be changed—different people, different markets. You and I won't be here. So what's the good of hurrying if you don't even have time to look at the sky?'"

The water grew quiet, and the air became light.

"He wants us to contemplate the eternal," I said. "But I think it's important to study people, too."

"It's that there's more to life than rushing around. We all need to take the time to rekindle the spark we hold inside us. And this," Max said, pointing upward, "helps keep things in perspective."

And so there we stood, a man and a woman at the high point of a bridge, alone in our island in time, dreaming of eternity.

The *trattoria* was festooned with colored lights the size of saucers. We stepped inside where an empty bar spanned the length of one wall and customers sat at clusters of cloth-covered tables. The diners resembled survivors of a shipwreck, water pooling on the floor around their boots, their sleeves dripping on the tables and their hair hanging in long, wet strands that looked like seaweed. The accordion player arrived ahead of us and was serenading a group in the corner with "*Luna mezza mare*" while a waiter with wild black brows led us to our seats and recited the specials.

Max glanced at the plastic-covered menu. "Ever try pasta cooked in squid ink?"

"Never." I wriggled out of my coat.

"Let's."

"And two glasses of house wine," I told the waiter. And to Max, "A pile of pasta plopped in a bowl of black sauce. I'm warning you, I might need both glasses."

"You exaggerate."

The waiter lit our candle, and as soon as he placed a basket of bread on the table, I tore a hunk and waved it in the air. "Bracing myself for black food."

"I've been meaning to ask, are you living in a film noir, or something?" Max rested his chin on his hands and looked me over.

"You haven't read my chapter on travel wear and black magic? It doesn't clash or show stains. It's slimming." I ticked off the plusses on my fingers. "And . . ."

"It's impenetrable?"

"I was about to say, it lets you to blend in with the crowd."

"It can also be interpreted as an outward sign of inner angst," Max said.

"On occasion."

The *pasta seppia* arrived. "I've never really eaten anything so . . ."

"Licorice?"

"Well, okay. But I feel like I should be dipping a *pen* in this, not a fork." I probed at the pasta immersed in cuttlefish ink, uncovering white rubbery chunks of squid that elicited an involuntary shudder.

Max twirled a forkful, spatter-painting the front of his sweater. "It's quite good."

"Uh-huh." I was finding it difficult to swallow. "Looks like you've been chewing carbon paper." He stuck out his tongue. "Yup."

"So we match." He flashed a ghoulish grin.

This was far worse than the deranged black-seeds-between-the-teeth look I'd achieved in Budapest when wolfing down a poppy seed muffin. I swished some wine around my mouth, bared my teeth, and hoped for the best.

"Oh, that's *much* better," he said, laughing.

The accordion player came to our table, playing "*Volare*." As he reached the *nel blu dipinto di blu* part, an Indian peddler hawking long-stemmed roses entered the dining room and was immediately summoned by a customer in the back. But in the middle of the transaction, the restaurant's owner rushed from the kitchen, yelling, "This is not *casa tua*. You come in here with your roses. You don't ask my permission." The proprietor lifted his eyebrows, gestured to one and all, and scooped air up from his aproned belly to his chest, as if to say,

See what I have to put up with? "Get out! *Via!*"

"What a grouch!" I said, under my breath.

Max caught the man as he exited, thrust some money into his hand, and took the remaining roses, presenting them to me. All this with such grace and good humor that the diners let out a collective "Ehhh." The peddler bowed and stepped out the door and into the night, with the accordion player on his heels.

"They've seen better days." Max said, lifting a limp flower with his finger.

"I love the sentiment," I said. "Thank you." Then we, too, abandoned the bright oasis for the damp alleyways where the musician lumbered ahead.

"*Scusi, signore!* Would you play something for us?" In the lamplight, the Ziplocs around Max's ankles glowed like jellyfish.

"*Cosa piace?*"

Max turned to me. "Claire?"

"*Con Te Partiro*," I said, pressing my face to the roses. As the musician's fingers moved along the keys, I leaned into Max, who sang: "I'll go with you . . ."

As he wrapped his arms around me, I chimed in, "Across seas that no longer exist."

The accordionist accepted Max's tip, wished us a *buona sera*, and slipped into an alley beside the Jewish Community Center. As we made our way toward the synagogue, I felt a sudden tilt in my chest when Max suggested that I stay the night.

"What about the rabbi, the congregation . . . my things at the hotel?"

"I can't see us wading to the Danieli tonight, can you? And me trying to make it back? I'll walk you to your hotel tomorrow."

"You're right. We'd only get wet and cold all over again."

"And they say business seminars are ruining the Danieli's charm anyway, so you won't be missing much."

Inside the dark apartment, I set the flowers on what I hoped was the table, pulled off my coat, and took a chair.

Max tugged at the sneakers. The wine, the music, the roses, and now his warm breath again on my knees . . . all went straight to my head, my heart, and

. . . Smother my knees with kisses and work your way up, I wanted to say.

"I'll take the pull-out sofa against the wall. The bed has a privacy curtain, but before you climb in, you'd better get in the shower to warm up." He handed me something soft, a tee shirt. "There's a robe on the bathroom door. I'm going to hunt for a vase."

When I lathered with the bar of soap, the warm, misty compartment filled with Max's woodsy fragrance. I stayed there a long time, reviving my chilled body. Then I dried off and put on the tee shirt, my panties, and the waffle-weave robe. After arranging my wet clothes on the heater, I emerged, steamy and sleepy, my adrenaline rush giving way to total relaxation.

"You look fantastic."

"And how would you know?" I felt around for the curtain.

"I just sense it." Suddenly he pressed against me, giving me a salty kiss that made my knees weaken.

"Whoa," I said, grabbing him to keep from losing my balance.

"Here, take this." He folded my fingers around a glass. "I'm heading for the shower."

I groped for the edge of the bed, sipping the smooth sherry that warmed me all the way to my toes, and pulled the comforter up to my chin. My head, cradled by the soft pillow, spun to the sound of the shower's spray.

In the middle of the night, I woke to use the bathroom and on my way back to bed somehow bumped into a corner of the sofa. Max's gentle snoring shifted.

"Oops, sorry," I whispered, pulling the curtain closed. I lay quiet, picturing the cottage scene from *It Happened One Night* where Clark Gable hangs a blanket, that he refers to as the Wall of Jericho, between twin beds.

"Claire?" Max sounded wide awake. "Could I come over for a minute?" He didn't wait for an answer, but slid in beside me, his bare chest pressed against my arm. And the walls came tumbling down. As Claudette watched Clark undress, her nipples peeped from beneath her lacy camisole. My own nipples stiffened as Max pulled me toward him, his mouth on my neck. "Thought this might be a good time," he said into the darkness.

"Hmm?"

"I haven't filled you in on Ruskin." I waited, silent, barely breathing, wanting to be filled in. The utter absence of light was liberating. Gone was the cellulite, replaced by scent and touch. "Thing is, he was into curves," Max said, caressing my hip with the palm of his hand. "The curl of a wave." Gentle kisses on my ear and throat. "Planets in orbit." He kissed my closed eyes. My toes tingled, the back of my neck prickled. When his hand pressed on the small of my back, my body throbbed with longing. He pulled me closer and gave me a long, long kiss on the mouth. "The prow of a boat, cleaving the water."

I felt hypnotized. "I'm getting the idea," I mumbled.

"Are you?"

I felt his tongue in my mouth, tasted the salt. That ended the tutorial on Ruskin. What followed was a series of effortless acts that felt inevitable, so natural they left me floating like Venice on Adriatic waters in the middle of a star-spangled night. Weightless. Shimmering like a phosphorescent creature, smelling of the sea.

11

Porta aperta per chi porta; e chi non porta, parta.
Bring something and the door opens; bring nothing and out you go!

The Italians refer to their shutters as *gli scuri,* because when they're closed every bit of noise and light disappears, but the instant Max threw them open, the apartment filled with blinding light and a chorus of voices. I pulled on my robe to join him at the window, spotted several backpacked teens surrounding a rumpled tour guide who was pointing in our direction, and immediately retreated.

"What on earth did you do, hang a banner?"

"A small one. I'm surprised they can see it from down there."

"No!"

"No, it's the plaque beside our window commemorating Jews who died in the Holocaust," Max said, his tone more serious.

Now that the room was full of light, I looked around for the paperweight that Isabella had bought at the Guggenheim gift shop, suspicious all along that it had been for Max. But all I found was a single dried rose. I picked it up.

"From that morning in the piazza," he said.

"You kept it." I twirled to the bed.

Max turned toward me, the morning light outlining his hair, shoulders, arms. "Kept it? I slept with it on my pillow every night. The glittering sea," he sang, "silver stars in your hair . . . " He prowled around the bed and lunged for me, kissing my stomach. "Last night, last night . . . Oh, Claire."

"Max," I said, squeezing him.

The rumpled bed was like an open book, the blanket's corner dog-eared to signify, "This is my favorite part." A single white pillow feather drifted to the floor.

He took me in his arms and kissed me. "One, two, three, four, five," he said, as his lips touched my forehead, eyes, nose and mouth.

Then we tumbled into bed and made love once more.

The water, having retreated to the canals and lagoon, left little sign of flooding. On our way to the *vaporetto*, we came across a young mother struggling to get her baby carriage up the stone steps of a bridge. Max spoke to her, and when she nodded, he took over, maneuvering the carriage with care and even making baby talk with the infant.

"My goal is to help a dozen people cross bridges before I leave."

"And how's that going?"

"Nearly halfway there." He smiled, counting on his fingers. "The Crooked Bridge, Bridge of Marvels, Bridge of Pots and Pans, Bridge of Swords, and now the Bridge of Spires."

"Maybe you could help *me* over a bridge."

"Glad to," he said, taking my hand in his.

The two Senegalese flashed smiles of recognition as they loped toward us with bundles of goods thrown over their backs, their glorious yellow sweaters glowing in the sunlight. And draped around their necks were the most beautiful hand dyed silk scarves, scarves that looked, on closer examination, very familiar.

"Nice to see you again, and where did you ever find these?" I said, admiring their newly acquired accessories.

"Angel," said the taller of the two. "The angel gave them to us."

"Angel?" I said. "Lovely." While I spent my time encountering ghosts, my friends from Senegal were accepting gifts from heavenly beings that had somehow retrieved Bernie's belongings from the lagoon and repurposed them.

Max and I boarded the *vaporetto*, my heart vaulting as we made our way along the Grand Canal. I never tired of the sight: palaces in hues of dusty rose, terra cotta, and burnt sienna springing from the brackish water, a fleeting vision of filigreed balconies, pointed arches, mullioned windows, and private docks marked by striped poles. All these colors and images swirled in the green waters, along with clumps of wavering clouds and celestial blue. Venice was a water lily, less seen than reflected. Max and I huddled in the stern, watching the sky and sea expand until the city's panorama grew so small that it belonged in one of Cornell's boxes.

"Someone should write a song like 'Santa Lucia' for Venice," said Max. "The golden sun, the silver moon, the blue Adriatic. It's got everything—the Doge's Palace, the campanile, Saint Mark's, and of course, the boats bobbing on the water. *Si, Madonna mia!*"

I laughed and kissed his cheek that the wind, pungent with salt and seaweed, had reddened. After most of the passengers debarked at the Lido, our boat chugged onward to Burano, and we watched a series of small islands drift by.

"Ruskin compared them to handfuls of jewelry scattered on a mirror."

"More Ruskin?" I nuzzled his neck, nibbled his earlobe.

As we drew closer to the shoreline, designs in bright mosaics caught the sunlight. The fishermen's houses were washed in wild combinations of blaring blue and atomic tangerine. Rubber boots dangled in pairs from cadmium yellow shutters. Open umbrellas hung from lime-green window boxes. And through each kitchen window, clusters of shiny copper and brass pots hung from wrought-iron hooks. All of which may have prompted a remark once made by Josie: "Venice may be the bride of the Adriatic, but Burano's a kitchen slut."

A kerchiefed woman in a long skirt and rolled-up sleeves sat among some fishing nets stretched out to dry against a church wall. As she mended, she sang in a scratchy voice, "*Come sei bella*, how beautiful you are." At the lace-making school, we stepped around a small girl who sat in the doorway, cheering two snails as they slimed across a crayoned drawing. The narrow stairs led us to an open room of women sitting in rows, cradling pillows, their hands busy with bobbins.

When we emerged onto Via Baldassare Galuppi, a woman tending a stand of linens and lace waved a doily in our direction. "*Punta in aria*, stitches in the air!" She beckoned to Max and pressed the gossamer piece into his hand, saying in Buranese sing-song, "Our lace has a story."

"Uh-oh," Max whispered into my hair.

"*C'era una volta*, long ago, a young Buranese left his beloved to find work in the Orient." Her steady gaze moved from Max's face to mine, and back again. "As he sailed the Indian Ocean, the sirens tried to bewitch him with their songs, but he did not succumb, no matter how they tempted him. So impressed by his faithfulness was the queen of mermaids that she wished to reward him. She swished her tail against the side of the ship and stirred the foam into a bridal veil. And that is how our lace came to be the most delicate on earth." I wondered if this story resonated with Max. Could he possibly avoid the sirens and impress me with his faithfulness?

In late afternoon, as we made our way to the boat landing, the vision of beautiful women dressed in dull red and brown standing in doorways and holding their sleepy babies gave the impression that all the Madonna paintings in Venice came alive every evening at dusk, in Burano.

On our boat ride back, a young woman stood alone at the prow like a figurehead, her windblown hair a Day-glo orange.

"She looks just like the actress in a movie I saw with my friend Roberto. He's a film historian and always has interesting insights."

"He lives on the Canal, in the pink palace?"

Max nodded. "Isabella's husband." My heart stirred. "This movie had different endings, depending on whether the woman jumps over a dog or dodges a car."

"I love the way movies expand our worlds. But it's not just that; it's sitting in the darkened room, being drawn into the big screen. That's one reason Bernie said he fell for me—my passion for movies. Later he told me that, more than anything else, it's what really got on his nerves."

"Something like that happened to me with the secretary of our department. Karen said she loved me for my free spirit. Then she wanted to keep me boxed in."

"So you ended the relationship?"

"We see each other around school, and that made it awkward at first. It got easier when she began dating someone else. Then they broke up. Once in a while we'll meet for coffee, as friends."

"Friends?"

"Yeah. I'm not one of those guys who believes friendship with a woman is impossible."

Josie and I shared a lot of theories about relationships. When Max mentioned his free spirit, Josie's words echoed in my ear: A huge mistake we women make with a new love interest is to fall for the twenty-five percent that really clicks and then lie to ourselves that, in time, we'll be able to change the other seventy-five percent to our liking. This faulty math leads to heartache and falls squarely within the realm of Foolish Things.

"Isn't it amazing how life revolves around chance," I said, still thinking about the movie Max had mentioned. "Bernie wanted a jacket from this shop that was closed for renovation, so we ended up at Eric's. And that was that."

I gazed at the lagoon, as stippled and streaked as the marbled paper the Venetians call *marmorizzata*, the kind used in the antique books filled with tales of love, the oldest stories in the world.

"Like you and me," I said. "Pure chance."

"With you, I feel I can be myself."

"And I feel, it's all so fast, I . . . "

"You what?"

"I'm breathless. I want you, but I'm afraid," I said.

"Ye-es." An arched eyebrow.

"I need to know you better."

"Oh, we can take care of that," Max said, giving my hand a gentle squeeze. "Ask me anything."

"Hmm, let me think." I wanted to ask him what he found attractive about me. I wanted to ask him about the depth of his feelings. I wanted to ask him if he could imagine a future together. Instead, I said, "How would you like to visit one of my favorite Madonnas?"

We ordered baby squid and prawns at the popular Alla Madonna, near the Rialto Bridge.

"No swing," our rosy-cheeked waiter advised a customer as he slid the pocket door to the ladies' room open for her in one fluid motion then breezed on by, balancing his tray. In Venice, exterior doors open inward to accommodate floods, while others slip into pockets like letters in envelopes. And some doors are *tromp l'oeil*—not doors at all. One of my favorite cartoons was of a lumpy, bespectacled boy pushing at a door clearly marked PULL while a sign above the entrance reads "School for the Gifted." So much in life depends on getting your foot in the door. And before you can do that, you have to see that the door exists. But sometimes we're so fixated on the closed door that we don't see the open one. Musset used this proverb as a title—a door must be open or shut—*ouverte ou fermée*. I wanted to focus on the open door.

"How'd you get into art history?" I said, once our waiter had taken our orders.

"When I was five, my parents took me to the Museum of Fine Arts in Boston and I thought we had entered a giant's castle." As he described the massive floral arrangements, Max pirouetted with his hands, nearly slapping the diner behind him. "Staircases that climbed forever. A café. And best of all, the gift shop."

"C'mon! What about the *art*?"

"I wasn't ready for it. A couple of years later . . . That's when the paintings were there for me. It was scary, the way I tumbled into them as if they were wells. My folks took an audio tour of the Monet exhibit, and I followed them from haystack to haystack, hypnotized. And then some guy wearing earphones turned to his wife, not realizing he was speaking at high volume, and blurted out, 'They all look like bran muffins to me!' That broke the spell. But not for long." Max leaned in and lowered his voice, as if to share a secret. "Because in the next room, I saw Venice through Monet's nearly blind eyes. Lagoons strewn with rose petals. Gondolas like curled leaves, fallen and floating.

"I was exhausted and getting cranky, so my father gave me a ride on his shoulders where I got an even better view. On the way home, we stopped at a drive-in for ice cream. I was leaning forward, chattering about the Monet paintings, and dripped melting ice cream down my father's shoulder. Cleanliness is one of my mother's obsessions, so she grabbed napkins and hurried to clean up the mess. But my Dad only joked that it was abstract art in the making."

"For me it began in grade school, with the explorers. Then there was a revival of *Lawrence of Arabia*. O'Toole's eyes were blue pools in the burning desert," I said, scooping up the last baby squid. "The music, the adventure really moved me. That's when I knew I'd travel to exotic places."

We left Alla Madonna and were walking in the direction of the Danieli Hotel when Max stopped in front of a pharmacy and said, "Hold on a minute. I'll be right back." He dashed into the store and returned with a plastic bag. "I bought us a present."

I peered inside at the supersized package of condoms. "Gee, thanks." Blushing, I pushed back a wave of worry that crashed against the wall of my chest. We hadn't used any protection last night or this morning.

We reached the Danieli. At the doorway to Room Ten, a potted palm rustled dry as old crinoline when my elbow brushed against it.

As I slid my key into the lock, Max said, "The two lovebirds stayed here, Sand and the French poet, right?"

"*I adore you. My pen is drunk with love,*" I quoted Musset. "He was such a romantic!" The door clicked open. "Later, though, they had problems. She was ten years older."

"There had to be more to it than that," he said, kissing my hair.

We sat by the tall window framed in rich satiny Fortuny and let the complimentary chocolate truffles melt in our mouths. The glow of the opalescent lampshade carried me back in time until I was able to see the sky through Musset's eyes—a variable taffeta of pink and blue. When the lovers parted, Sand cut off her hair and sent it to him, a desperate act. But I didn't want to dwell on misery or obsess about age differences. I didn't want every word from my mouth echoing references to some writer or painter. I was tired of having my soul replaced by thoughts and feelings that belonged to others. It was time to trust in myself. It's just that sometimes . . .

"Jeanne Moreau stayed here, too," I said. "Don't you love her mouth?" There, I did it again.

"I love *your* mouth."

Max took the plastic bag from my hand and broke open the jumbo box.

Then he kissed my eyelids and whispered, "Your eyes, your nose . . . " His breath tickled my ear. He undressed me and lifted me to the desk, its worn surface cool against my skin.

Cupping my bottom to keep me close, he entered me slowly, waited for me to arch my back and thrust my pelvis forward. Time expanded and extended, a strand of sweet taffy pulled to a slender golden thread that broke as I left myself, left my body, and passed through Heaven's gate.

We slept in late, and when we went downstairs, the lobby bustled with a bevy of platinum blondes who mingled while their tuxedoed escorts waited on the sidelines. A placard in pink letters read, "Top Producers of Mary Kay."

"Wonder if a gondola's been painted pink just for them," I said.

"What did I tell you . . . seminars," Max said. He grabbed my bag, and we left the Danieli, arriving in minutes at the Londra, also on the Riva Schiavoni. "I don't get it," he said as a doorman greeted us. "Why restrict yourself to these posh and predictable places?" I checked in at the front desk. "World class and five star. How about a hostel, or a rental in a synagogue?"

"I want to serve my readers," I said. And to feel safe in predictable surroundings.

"What about B&Bs?" Max said. "Your readers could enjoy the same views for a fraction of the cost."

"La Calcina's considered a B&B."

"I think you're following *too* closely in the footsteps of others. Look at your friend . . . "

"Josie?"

"You say she loves her apartment, gets to know her neighbors. Moving around like this, doesn't it all become a blur after a while?"

"It *can* suspend a sense of reality."

"And responsibility," Max said.

"Such as having no condoms during a flood?" There, I had finally put into words what was being left unsaid, that I advise travelers to carry condoms at all times. Fill them with ice as an emergency pack, I tell them, or put a leaky tube of shampoo in one and tie a knot to seal it, or, well, the obvious.

"I thought you'd hand me one at the right time," Max laughed.

"So you're saying it was *my* responsibility."

"Not exactly, but . . . " He was no longer smiling.

This sounded like the beginning of a fight. "Tchaikovsky composed his Fourth Symphony in this room," I said, opening the door.

Max looked around. "There's an Internet connection. Mind if I call the desk for a laptop?"

While he wrote to his parents, I dozed on the same bed that Tchaikovsky had slept and dreamed in. And when I awoke, Max was asleep beside me. I studied the stubble on his chin, the shadows cast by his thick lashes. As I listened to him breathing, I began to drift off again. But then he kissed me and pulled me toward him.

"Not now," I said. "How about a nice bath?"

We slid into the frothy bubbles, my back up against his chest. He soaped my shoulders and spine, pressing down in little circles until I loosened up and relaxed my body against his.

"Seems like a lifetime ago I stopped over at Frankfurt-am-Main and searched everywhere for a lousy bottle of water," Max said. "Now here I am, surrounded by it."

I closed my eyes, remembering early morning stopovers at the airport: baggy-eyed smokers drooping at tiny tables supported by chrome tubes, the workers in blue coveralls scooting on bicycles from gate to gate, a German police dog in a vest marked "*Zoll*" sniffing at a pile of luggage.

"A strange feeling creeps over me when I'm at the airport that my whole life has been filmed and there I am, at Judgment City, halfway between this life and some higher plane. Like the set in *Defending Your Life*."

Max poured water on my hair. "It wouldn't change the way *I* do things." He worked the shampoo in.

"If your life were being recorded, and judged?"

"You mean it *isn't*?" Yiddish accent again.

I moved down so he could reach the top of my head. "I've never run into a burning house, like Streep did in the movie," I said. "I *have* played the flute for the Salvation Army until my lips turned blue."

"Better cover your eyes." He rinsed my hair.

"Unless, let's see now . . . helping a gay guy try out heterosexual life counts? The sad story of my marriage, recently terminated." I brushed bubbles from my chin. "Brooks is sentenced to go back to earth because he's not qualified to move on."

Max's hand rested at the base of my neck. "That's troubling," he said in a gruff voice.

"But he manages to jump from his tram and races to the one carrying Streep."

"No, I'm talking about your husband hooking up with some guy."

"Well, yes. That took some getting used to."

"What I'm saying is that he wasn't monogamous. He was fooling around. And now you and I have had unprotected sex." Max got out of the tub and helped me up. He toweled my back and shoulders.

"I'm sorry." My voice caught with emotion. "I didn't even think. How could I have been so stupid?" I could only hope that meticulous Bernie had been more careful than I had been.

"We'll get it checked out, but there's no sense worrying about it now." Max wrapped a towel around me, and reached for a second one. "So . . . does Brooks catch his train?"

I nodded. "The one headed to Heaven. He clings to the door, and pounds and screams until they let him in."

"Passion-driven." Max towel-dried my hair. "*And* a rule-breaker. I can relate."

Max led me to Tchaikovsky's bed where we made love. Then we took a bath. Then we made love. Who needed to catch a tram anywhere? This was Heaven on Earth.

12

Tra il dire e il fare niente traghetti.
There's no ferry that runs between saying and doing.

"A tribute to Tchaikovsky and his Fourth Symphony, the 'Two Lions,'" I said, as we entered the Do Leoni restaurant where lions were woven into the carpet and carved in the English furniture.

"My birth sign," Max said, as we followed the maitre d' to our table. "Not that I pay much attention to horoscopes." A waiter whisked linen napkins from the table to our laps. "You may as well read a stone."

"Cards and constellations, maybe," I said. "But a *stone*?"

"Find one you feel good about."

"Last time I did that I was in second grade, playing hopscotch."

Max placed a sugar cube in his palm. "Go ahead, ask it a question. Something important."

"Like, will you sweeten my coffee? Or, be a building block in my miniature igloo?"

"Don't give me hard time." The waiter smirked when he returned to find Max interrogating the sugar cube. We placed our orders, baked salmon with truffles for him, *bigoli* with scampi and red sauce for me.

"Does it have to be a yes or no, like questions to the oracle at Delphi?"

"You're looking for more than that. Stones have faces." He turned the cube and handed it to me. "And each face holds part of the answer. It's up to you to put it together."

"Okay, here goes. Is it time to eat, or what?" I asked the small white cube before popping it into my mouth.

When our meals arrived, I sampled the rough, thick pasta. "Hmm. This sauce really sticks. Still, it doesn't compare to Chef Nicolò's."

"They say *bigoli's* slang for 'penis,'" Max said.

"Hadn't heard that one." Realigning my knife and spoon, I wondered who "they" might be. I gazed out the window at an equestrian statue ringed with lion-taming women. What would it take, I wondered, to tame a lion?

"That reminds me," he said. "I want a closer look at the statue at the Guggenheim. You know, the one by the water." Marini's *Angelo della città* is a modern equestrian with outstretched arms, and an outstretched *bigolo*. "I wonder, is the penis really detachable?" Max dug into his salmon. "There's a story that Peggy unscrewed it and asked some art forger to hold it while she kissed him. His reaction was, 'Sorry, mine's not nearly this hard.'"

I struggled to swallow my water without sputtering it all over.

"Poor Peggy," I said, after composing myself. "She was furious with men. She said that while they were sleeping with her, what they really wanted to do was to sleep with the other men she was sleeping with. Is that twisted?"

"It *does* sound complicated. Anyway, I'm pretty busy for the next few days," Max said in a detached way, "and I imagine you have work to do. So I'll give you a call."

Alone in bed the next morning, I stared past the Biedermeier furniture at generous portions of sky served up by the pair of tall windows. One framed clear blue with a trace of cirrus clouds, collections of minute ice crystals at twenty thousand feet, and the other, black and white in a blender. Gray. As if the windows were offering me a choice. Max was fun, impulsive, and it was wonderful making love with him. But I had the sobering thought that I probably played a small part in the overall picture called his life. I was expected to be carefree and available when convenient.

I went downstairs and found a message from Michael at the front desk. He answered his cell on the first ring, said he was free until mid-afternoon and was interested in visiting a Murano glass factory. I brushed aside all thoughts of Max and asked Michael to meet me in the lobby, then grabbed a cup of coffee at the bar.

Michael didn't come across as a bland dish this morning. Dressed in casual pants and a smashing sweater, I noted a deep dimple on his cheek that appeared whenever he smiled. And thinking back, we were having a great time the other day until I spotted Max at The Bunch of Grapes and read the proverb about appetite and sauce on that damned beam. Michael took my hand as we walked the few steps to the lagoon that lapped and shimmered, and caught the boat to Murano.

"I was worried about you during the flood, even called your room to check on you, but they said they hadn't seen you."

"No, I was out that evening and couldn't make it back, so I stayed with a friend."

"Josie?"

Better to answer a question with a question. "Did *you* get caught in the flood?"

"I was safe and sound in my room."

Seagulls wheeled overhead as the *vaporetto* carried us toward the outlying island and away from the "pearl of the Adriatic." It seemed to me, as we sailed farther out, that with its play of colors and iridescence, Venice was more like an opal, the stone believed to cure diseases of the eye. We docked and, within minutes, were standing at the entrance of a working glass furnace.

"Tenth-century," Michael said, reading from the sign.

"Any glassmaker who tried to leave the island was threatened with death. That's how secret the craft was."

We entered the large stone building where, with a twist, a turn, and a push of the craftsman's breath, the molten glob of glass on the end of a hollow iron rod was transformed into a bird.

"For centuries, Murano specialized in mirrors," said the guide. "Later enameled glass, crystalline. Colored glasses were created to resemble gemstones." I glanced at Michael. Was he colored glass or gem?

The guide told us that the furnaces stopped manufacturing the type of glass that flew to pieces on contact with poison so that the sale of cheap wine could continue.

"He didn't mention the Murano dagger, used by assassins in the Middle

Ages," I told Michael. "They'd bury the blade in the victim and snap the handle off."

"Leaving no sign of a serious injury?"

"Exactly."

"The walking wounded," he said. "I'm afraid I've fallen among their ranks."

"If I told you I had, too, would you see me . . . "

"As somehow less?" He took my hand again.

"As a sweater with a serious pull." A smile tugged at the corners of my mouth.

"Hardly, Claire. We're like that hot glass. Caught at the right time, our lives can be shaped to suit our dreams." My hand felt warm in his.

"Someone told me that the divorce doesn't make me more vulnerable, just more open to change."

"You see? But before looking for love, we have to break down the barriers we've built against it."

Michael gave me a light kiss on the lips when we parted in front of the Londra. I watched him make his way along the promenade. A kind man, thoughtful, wise. When I sifted through my feelings for Michael, I became the conflicted woman at the café. "He pleases me, yet he doesn't please me." He was dependable. Check. I was terrified of building a relationship with someone that I was beginning to count on. Check.

In the morning, I was awakened by a call from Gianni, the art dealer.

"I've been too busy to call sooner, but I thought today you might accompany me to Torcello. Meet me at the dock in an hour, and we can take a look at the Byzantine Madonna."

"It's short notice, but fine." I dressed in a hurry and met Gianni at the landing to catch the boat for the remote island.

"Torcello was wiped out centuries ago by malaria," Gianni said, the wind whipping his thin hair. "Rifled for its stone and statues, left only with a few decrepit houses."

As we debarked and followed the path from the landing stage, I sensed an absence of any spirits. In Venice, I encountered Lord Byron in the piazza, Proust at the Quadri, both eager to dish out advice. Then there was the timid

Cornell, the agitated Tintoretto and the dour Ruskin. But this desolate island didn't have much to lure a ghost, never mind entice one to linger.

"Ponte del Diavolo," Gianni said, as we came to an ancient bridge without a parapet. "They say the Devil takes the first soul to cross it."

"Then by all means," I said, "lead the way."

"I cross this bridge many times, believe me. Tourists come into my shop, run their fingers over the antiques and they leave. But a year ago a friend from Naples suggested a partnership. He helped turn my business into a lucrative one."

We continued single file along a reed-lined route that led to the campanile. After taking the crumbling stairs to the top, Gianni pointed to remnants of canals filled with silt, old foundations, and paths that led nowhere.

"Historians tell us that Venice was settled by those fleeing Attila," he said, "but the truth is fishermen were already living here along the shore, like seabirds in their nests of twigs." His breath reeked of garlic.

As I stood there dreaming of the island picnic that Ruskin and Effie enjoyed during their holiday in 1850, I could almost see them savoring their *panini* and wine as they watched the boats pass down the ancient canal. Gianni surprised me by putting his arm around me, and when I pushed him away, he simply shrugged.

"And now, on to the *Madonna Teotoca*," he said, his eyelid twitching.

We crossed the grass-covered piazza to the seventh-century church where Torcello's treasure glittered mystically on a background of pure gold.

"The noblest monument in the lagoon." Gianni stared at the elongated Byzantine Madonna.

"Forever sad, with that tear sliding down her face," I said.

A predatory look flickered over Gianni's neutral expression, as if given half a chance he'd gladly pry the silvery tear off and slip it into his pocket.

In the early 1900s, a guide thought nothing of casually chipping pieces of mosaic off the wall of the Doge's Palace with his knife and offering them for sale and, at the Acropolis, running up a workman's ladder to knock a carved leaf from a capital.

My face grew hot, thinking about precious goods, stolen, of my husband in the arms of a leather-clad thief whose face became a satyr's, then morphed into Gianni's. I pictured Gianni let loose in Saint Mark's, cannibalizing the *Pala d'Oro*. At his hands, the magnificent altarpiece decorated with six thousand jewels would end up looking like defective costume jewelry at a rummage sale. I felt like that damaged altarpiece, trust scraped off with a putty knife, treasured memories pried out with a screwdriver, love tossed to the ground. We walked the church grounds and arrived at a mound of stone resembling a dust-covered easy chair.

"Attila's throne. Make yourself comfortable, and I will return *subito*."

I waited there with shadows from the olive tree playing on my hands and face, lapsing into a reverie finally broken by the shriek of a gull, like a baby's cry. I watched as Gianni exited from one of the ramshackle houses in the distance, shaking hands with a man who stood in the dim doorway. Then he came toward me, struggling with two large shopping bags, wheezing and panting so much I feared for his sixty-year-old heart.

"Better slow down," I said.

"Don't worry about me! My latest acquisitions!" He lifted the bags, adjusting his grip.

"Not from the *island*?" I said, fearing the worst.

"No, no," he said, averting his gaze. "Statues of Isis and Horus were unearthed here twenty years ago." Then he locked his swamp-colored eyes on me. "But there's not been much since."

As Gianni left me at the steps of the hotel, he turned and said, almost as an afterthought, "Permit me to come to your room around eight this evening? I'll bring along an important artifact for your pleasure." He looked at the pavement, the top of his bald head tilting toward me.

"I'm basically here for the Madonnas," I reminded him. The wind lifted long strands of gray hair from his comb-over.

"I've kept that in mind, *certamente*," he said.

Foolish Thing: I ignored the feeling of threat in the pit of my stomach.

When he arrived that night, Gianni reeked of cheap wine and musky cologne, a scent that triggered memories of an afternoon in the Amherst

Pharmacy when Josie sprayed our wrists with a tester and joked about the saddle on the label of the all-purpose Old English used by the college boys. More powerful than anything, even music, smell delivers whole scenes back from memory. If scent is an ant, then memory is the large crumb that it carries.

Gianni, with a tuft of grizzled hair sprouting from his open-necked shirt, settled into a soft chair by the French windows. He crossed his legs, gray-green pants shining and scales on his reptilian shoes catching the light. I opened a bottle of Lacrima Christi, poured us each a glass, and thought about the Madonna dell'Orto's missing Bellini.

When Gianni pulled a small cloth package from his bag and unwrapped an ancient bearded horse-tailed satyr holding a wine cup and sporting a stiff *bigolo*, I said, "That doesn't look like a Madonna to me. What's its provenance?"

He raised one eyebrow, filled his glass to the brim, and topped mine. Then he grabbed for my hand, but I stood up abruptly, spilling my drink. It seeped into the linen tablecloth.

"Excuse me, Gianni." Swilling his drink, he continued to leer at me as I headed for the bathroom. I turned the lock and spent some time splashing cold water on my face. Then I straightened up, patted my face with a towel, and opened the door to find all the lights turned off.

"You have *got* to be kidding," I shouted, every muscle clenching.

Out of the darkness he came lunging, ramming his mouth onto mine like a *vaporetto* slamming against a landing stage. With the herky-jerky motion of a hand-held camera, he knocked me backward onto the bed. In the dim light seeping through the bathroom entryway, I noticed his thin hair rose up as if by a sudden wind gust. An elbow to the head pushed him away. That's when I saw it, an orange glow-in-the-dark party condom bobbing toward me.

"For God's sake, where are your pants?" I jumped off the bed, shouting, "*Vecchio schifoso!*" I grabbed the vase on the console and brought it down on his head. "*Cretino!*" I growled, kicking at the orange baton.

"Signora Claire!" he pleaded.

I whipped the door open and shoved Gianni into the carpeted hallway where he tripped, his hands cupping his deflated balloon. I flicked on the lights, packed up his ancient artifact and his pants and threw those out, too.

Then I double locked my door and jammed a *quattrocentro* chair against the knob. My hands shook as I collapsed on the bed.

Memo to Myself: Include a stronger cautionary note in my next book for the single female traveler.

A hot shower with tons of suds and serious scrubbing with a loofah made me feel a whole lot better. It was nice to know that I was still in good enough shape to fight off such imbeciles. I placed an anonymous call to the *carabinieri*, supplying the name and address of Gianni's shop and a description of the artifact. I hinted that Gianni might be involved in marketing stolen goods. Call it my note in the lion's mouth.

In the morning, I checked out of the Londra and moved to the Hotel Gritti where my room was graced not only with the usual gilt mirror and hand-painted dresser, but a view of the Canal and the domed Santa Maria della Salute. Best of all was the box-spring bed set in a curtained nook that gave a protected and, at the same time, sexy feel, like the bed at Max's apartment. I climbed in and took a long nap, dreaming of the Madonna, confident and serene, as she watched my every move.

13

Partire è un po' morire.
To part is to die a little.

"Peggy called this place home," Max said as we toured the Guggenheim. "And actually wandered out in her jammies for morning coffee?"

"Some people know how to live."

We entered the room where Max Ernst's *Attirement of the Bride* was displayed. A green swan held a spearhead and menaced a red-cloaked three-headed bird-woman.

"Ernst called the swan 'Loplop,'" said Max. "His private phantom."

"Do you have any phantoms?" I said.

"I think we all do. I'm haunted by images of some of my family dying in concentration camps. And my mother suffers from having been a child of survivors. But I work at confronting my demons."

"About your mother . . . that must be difficult," I said. I ached for my own parents, often talked aloud to them, but my phantoms weren't frightening or depressing. Ernst's ugly green swan, on the other hand, reminded me of my nasty experience with Gianni the night before, but I was reluctant to tell Max about it.

"It can be a struggle. The rabbi says she's caught in an inner Egypt where her slave masters keep her from becoming who she's supposed to be. But she's got family and friends." Max leaned to read a small plaque on the wall next to the painting. "Ernst escaped the Gestapo and wanted to see the world with closed eyes to reach a higher truth."

"In that case, I'm keeping *my* eyes *open*."

We walked out to the front lawn so that Max could examine the angel sculpture from every angle. "This is what I'd rather focus on, the uplifting. And he's one enthusiastic guy, wanting to hug the city . . . and make love with it, too." After running his hand along the horse's neck, Max grasped the base of the angel's penis with both hands and tried to unscrew it.

"Maaax!" I clutched his wrist and glanced around. "Keep this up and they'll be leading us over the Bridge of Sighs."

"Just wanted to know if the stories were true," he said, releasing his grip.

"I can see the headlines now, 'U.S. art historian molests treasured sculpture!' Come on, let's go!" I led him back inside the museum, and although I had planned to introduce him to Cornell's work, decided instead to walk him briskly out the exit.

"Max, I want to tell you something," I said, as we strolled along the canal. "It's not a big deal, but last night I made the mistake of letting someone into my room, and . . . "

Max stopped in his tracks. "*What?* Are you serious?"

"Don't worry," I said, "I called the police."

"The *police*? What the hell happened, Claire?"

"Well, this piece on the Madonnas . . . "

"What *happened*?"

"I let this antiquities dealer in, and the next thing I knew, the lights were off and so were his pants."

"I can't believe it. What were you thinking . . . letting a stranger into your room? Jesus, Claire! Did he hurt you?" Max clenched his fists.

"No. Shook me up a little, but mostly I'm angry," I said. "He wasn't exactly a stranger. He's a contact I've used in the past. I had no idea he could be such a sleaze." I wanted to say, "Don't blame the victim," but Max had a point. What *had* I been thinking?

"God, I'd like to get my hands on him!"

"What's more, I'm sure he's dealing in stolen art."

"Damn!" he said, his face flushed. "I'm just glad you're okay. It's baffling how you can be so cautious about some things and other times you seem . . .

self-destructive."

"I think you're overstating," I said, but I knew he was right.

"Let's say a bit reckless, then." He pulled me close, and we continued our walk with matching strides. "The good thing is you're safe. And if anyone can recover art, it's the Italians. They've found works by Raphael, Tintoretto, Tiepolo, and recently a Giorgione was rescued from an abandoned convent off the Greek coast." As we continued along the canal, I noticed that the hawker of watercolors wasn't at his usual post.

"What about the painting from the Madonna dell'Orto?" I said, remembering the empty easel.

"Not yet. But they *have* found a Bellini missing for thirty years in the possession of a Russian art dealer in Switzerland."

"So there's hope."

"Oh, yeah. The Artistic Heritage Protection Squad, they call themselves. They've recovered art worth millions, most of it stolen, if you can believe this, from the Vatican. There's so much art there, it's impossible to catalogue it all. But that's nothing compared to your safety, Claire."

"The whole incident was more laughable than anything."

"You're lucky." Our footsteps echoed along the ancient alley as we headed to Planet Internet.

At the computer, Max let out a groan. "My mother's been admitted to the hospital."

"Can I do anything?"

"Wait while I arrange for an earlier flight." His fingers flew across the keys. "There's one with Lufthansa at six-thirty tonight. Doesn't give me much time." He checked his watch. "Sorry about this, Claire."

"I'm sorry, too. Let me come with you to get your things. I'd like to ride with you to the airport."

I realized that my world was shifting quickly. Max packed everything into his one carry-on while I tidied up the apartment, took the dishes from the drying rack and stacked them in the cupboard. Before we left, he knocked on the rabbi's door and said goodbye.

From the Piazzale Roma we took a shuttle bus along the Ponte della Libertà causeway that tethered the fish-city to the mainland. The skies were clear, and when we arrived at Marco Polo, the airport was busy. Everything was rush rush, with no time for making concrete plans about the future.

"I'll be in touch," were his last words before he disappeared behind security gates.

On the ride back, I stared out the bus window and felt abandoned, so at a corner bar, I comforted myself with a glass of Montepulciano. Every time a regular left, the others would call in unison, "*Ci vediamo domani.*" I wanted someone to say they would see *me* tomorrow, but I consoled myself that as soon as I returned to Newburyport, Max and I would get together.

I hugged myself against the cold and passed vendors surrounded by fragrant clouds of cinnamon as they tended kettles of hot mulled wine. Others roasted chestnuts and stashed apples in coal scuttles, turning the fruit to warm pudding.

"*Vin brulé, marrone, mele!*" they called.

That night *bambini* were well bundled and everyone was preceded by white blossoms of frosty breath as the starry heavens slowly pin-wheeled above.

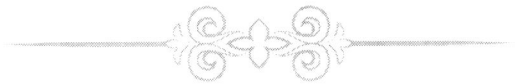

14

Sposi bagnati, sposi fortunati.
Wet newlyweds, lucky newlyweds.

Missing Max, I returned to the synagogue where the heavy green shutters of his apartment were closed and locked. The atmosphere in the Old Ghetto was silent and drab until a group of young children wearing paper crowns and capes poured from the public school into the *piazzetta*. They lined up, banging on pots and pans with their wooden spoons. When their teacher hoisted a horse of papier maché, they chanted "*San Martino, San Martino,*" and down the alley they marched, their happy sounds ringing along the walls, until they reached the Canal. High tide lapped at the cobblestones and soaked the shoes of vendors selling fish while indulgent adults dropped coins, candy, and cookies into small, open hands.

Making my way to Piazza San Marco, I held the image of the children in my mind and imagined the joys of scrubbing an upturned little face, packing a lunch, recounting the story of Saint Martin. Apart from a Baroque tune that drifted from the Quadri Café, the square was unusually quiet. Everyone had gathered at the Grand Canal to view the spectacle of a large wedding party coming ashore from gondolas. I joined the throng, and like a child celebrating Saint Martin's Day, held my palm open for anything that might come my way, a few grains of rice, a flower petal, the sense of joy that filled the air.

Onlookers smiled and clapped as the cameras clicked. The best man had the newlyweds pose on the walkway and, trying for the best possible shot, suggested that they take a step backward. The bride's heel—and this was the moment when I recognized the bride as Yuan-Ling—caught in the pavement. She toppled backwards into the lagoon, her gown billowing like a peony in full bloom. As the groom jumped in after her, spectators and guests rushed to the water's edge. The air filled with screaming and yelling in Chinese and Russian.

"*Aiuto, aiuto!*" I called to the departing gondolier, "*I sposi* have fallen in the Canal. They're drowning!"

"*Petta! Petta!*" the boatman yelled. Wait, wait. And as he turned his vessel around, I saw that it was Angelo. Meanwhile, I pulled an oar from a moored gondola and held it out to the newlyweds to keep them from sinking to the bottom where discarded dishwashers, gondoliers' sunglasses, Islamic stoneware, and Renaissance shoes lay in a jumble. Yuan-Ling clung to the extended oar, and Stefan, his brand new wedding band glinting, rested his hands on her shoulders. When Angelo arrived and helped lift the couple from the water, the onlookers cheered and gave each other a slap on the back. The videographer continued silently to film as Angelo threw me a puzzled look that turned to one of recognition.

"You saved us," Yuan-Ling said.

"I helped."

"No, really. You offered us a lifeline while everyone else ran around in circles."

Stefan embraced me, and I realized that if my life were in fact being recorded, this scene would carry some weight in Judgment City.

Michael appeared from the crowd, saw that I was shivering, and wrapped me in his jacket. "You did a fantastic job, Claire. Are you all right?"

"I think it's the adrenaline rush," I said, my teeth chattering. "And then the relief that everything turned out okay."

"She drowns clothes," Angelo shouted, delighted to be recorded by the whirring camera, "and saves drowning *sposi! Brava donna!* We say wet newlyweds are happy ones, but this is too much!" Still the subject of the videotape, he removed his red scarf, called me over and made a big show of tying it around my neck and giving me a big, wet kiss—a gondolier's kiss. The applauding crowd cheered and yelped, "*Brava! Bravo!*"

"Here, have a seat," Michael said, leading me to a bench where he wrapped my icy fingers around a cup of hot chocolate. As the crowd dispersed, Angelo and Michael spoke in low tones.

"Claire, Angelo insists on taking us for a ride."

"Really?"

"I've never been in a gondola, and it would mean so much to me. He says he wants to take us beneath the Bridge of Sighs."

"Sounds nice," I said, warming up to the idea.

Once we boarded, Angelo offered me a crushed velvet lap blanket that Michael tucked around my knees, and as we glided up a side canal, Michael said, "Angelo, I'm curious. What did you mean when you said that Claire drowns clothes?"

And Angelo was only too happy to regale Michael with his version of that first day in Venice when I hurled Bernie's stylish wardrobe into the lagoon.

"But after Signorina Claire released some of her anger, I deposited my distinguished passenger at the Accademia Bridge and returned *subito* to collect everything. In these waters, littering is not permitted."

We drifted slowly along the Rio di Palazzo, and when we reached the point directly beneath the Bridge of Sighs, Angelo sang out, "Love and bliss if you kiss!" and Michael took me in his arms and kissed me. Love and bliss. Angelo didn't specify with whom, but I fit into Michael's arms perfectly. Our lips met so naturally. Warmth filled my body, and I felt . . . safe and sound.

That evening, I doubled up on sweaters and cruised the Canal on the *Numero Uno*, revisiting the timeworn façades and illuminated rooms. This trip had topped my experiences in Katmandu and Saigon, Peru and Cairo. Meeting Max, Michael, Daniela, and Nicole; defending myself against Gianni; and now, rescuing a drowning bride and groom. I couldn't help but wonder if I had been in the wrong places at the right time or in the right places at the wrong time. The thunderbolt. Who knew what was to come? Maybe everything was as it should be.

In the morning, a maid knocked at the door and entered with a large fruit tray. I carried it, along with a pitcher of water and shallow bowl for washing, out to the balcony where I rolled an apple in the clear water and polished it with a cloth napkin. I sat back, ate the fruit, and watched the activity of the watercraft on the Canal—police boats, grocery barges, gondolas, water taxis, and *vaporetti*. I considered what Max had suggested, that as glorious as these hotel rooms were, it might be time for me to explore alternatives. I ruled out a place that Josie recently described as more of a bohemian backpacker's hostel than a B&B, although the pasta dinner included in the room rate held some appeal. More attractive to me were those simple B&Bs, places with private gardens and rooftop terraces hidden from tourists, places where one was treated as a member of the family.

A sparrow came along, perched on the rim of my water bowl, took a sip, and then went for a full bath.

When I finally left my room, I stopped by the kitchen to say hello to Chef Nicolò, who was busy at the oven.

"Good morning, Chef."

"Ah, the famous heroine. Your picture is in this morning's *Gazzettino*, saving the newlyweds. A splendid thing to do! If you're going out for the day, you'd better take one of these." He wrapped a warm, fragile croissant in a napkin and handed it to me along with his copy of the newspaper.

"Mmm, delectable," I said, taking in the buttery aroma. Chef's expansive spirit, his empathy and generosity, moved me to give him a peck on the cheek. "*You* are delectable. Thank you."

On the *vaporetto* headed for the Lido, I read the *Gazz*'s front-page story. They ran the picture of Angelo giving the Americana a kiss. According to the article, Angelo had earned quite a reputation as a rescuer of objects accidentally dropped into the canals by tourists and locals. So I understood more fully his distress at having been asked to throw Bernie's clothes overboard. Performing such an act went completely against his nature and his reputation.

As part of the story, the reporter reminded readers that the popular gondolier had escaped death one rainy day only two weeks earlier, after retrieving a pair of glasses lost by a child. During a sudden downpour, rather than seek shelter under the balcony of the nearby palazzo, he chose to stand unprotected and have the rain rinse the saltwater from his wetsuit. As he stood there, he felt something like a slap on his shoulder when a twenty-pound block of marble hit the walkway, leaving only a white scrape like a chalk line on his wetsuit. It was a close call.

The swags of foam forming at the *vaporetto's* bow reminded me of the Buranese lace story and Yuan-Ling's wedding gown ballooning in the Canal. In a photographer's negative, the bride's dress would reverse to black, like the frock worn by Constance Fenimore Woolson—"Fenimore," as Henry James called her. The two writers traveled together, even lived together briefly, she yearning for more than James was able to deliver. In the end, she resided alone in Venice, working on a novel in which her character is saved from an attempted suicide. But with no one there to save *her*, Fenimore leaped from the window of her rented room to the walkway below.

After they burned bundles of her letters and personal papers, James and Fenimore's sister sorted through her belongings. Then he rented a gondola and lugged her fine dresses out into the lagoon, where he directed the gondolier to push them underwater. But the clothes resurfaced, pulsating in the moving water like large black jellyfish. After repeated tries the stubborn silks sank, along with a mosaic brooch that Fenimore had worn at her pale throat. Now the brooch rests somewhere on the lagoon's murky floor, not far from the spot where fishermen refuse to cast their nets, swearing the waters are haunted by the ghosts of prisoners tied in weighted sacks and heaved overboard.

Some speculate that one day tourists will travel by glass-bottomed boat, gaze into the lagoon, and catch fleeting views of the campanile and the domes of Saint Mark's. I remembered the afternoon Bernie and I drove to Quabbin, the largest man-made drinking water reservoir in the world.

"The state took it by eminent domain," Bernie said, looking out over the huge body of pristine water, "and flooded four towns. Families packed up their things, dug up their dead, and moved out." At the time, I imagined trout and salmon exploring a one-room schoolhouse. I imagined eels attending church, large-mouth bass rummaging in pantries. I imagined a tree root, a wall, a tombstone in New England's lost and watery world, its version of Atlantis. And then there were the ruins of the Pharos lighthouse of ancient Alexandria, thousands of pieces of columns, capitals, sphinxes, and statues submerged in the offshore waters of the Mediterranean. But the notion of all of Venice underwater was to me, well . . . unfathomable.

The Lido's wide boulevard allowed for cars, motorbikes, and buses, and because it was Saturday, the promenade provided for *la vida della strada*, the life of the streets. Venetians in shawls, pullovers, and woolen berets walked their dogs, greeted their friends, did some shopping, or grabbed a quick espresso. In honor of La Standa's branch opening, a young man in a suit offered me an orchid, its fragile fuchsia blossoms dancing in the brisk Adriatic breeze.

"*Grazie*," I said, reluctantly removing my hand from my coat pocket to accept the delicate flower. My fingers grew cold, and the fragile flower, like the Senegalese, clearly belonged in warmer climes. I walked to the Chiesa di San Nicolò and left the orchid with the Madonna painted by Palma the Elder, who depicted his women in soft tones, sensual and tender, with garments rich in color. Often he left a single breast exposed, a nipple peeking over a chemise, like Claudette's in *It Happened One Night*. But this Madonna was modestly clothed, and in spite of the child that wriggled in her arms, her face held a dreamy expression.

Leaving the church, I continued to the Hôtel des Bains, Thomas Mann's haunt and the inspiration for his novella in which the main character, Gustav, fed up with a life of restraint, yearned to explore his wild and, as it turned out, homosexual side. Problem was, he spent his final days as a prisoner of love. With his hair dyed black, his face powdered and penciled as if by a mortician, Gustav died of cholera.

If Max and I did end up together, would I need to spend the rest of my life working out at the gym, coloring my hair, investing in various nips and tucks to my face and body, trying in vain to dissolve those years that separated us? And what about Michael? The taste of his kiss still lingered on my lips. A turn onto Lungomare Marconi brought the looming Hôtel des Bains into view. Soon, its wide steps led me to a sweeping veranda.

It was a relief to get inside, away from the cold. Giving the desk attendant a friendly nod, I wandered through cavernous dining halls nearly as spacious as the rooms at the Doge's Palace. Mann had dined here among the sounds of Italian, German, and Polish spoken in hushed tones, silverware clinking and newspapers rustling.

In the restroom, hot water from the shiny brass faucet warmed my aching hands. I searched my bag for lip balm, buried somewhere beneath my bathing suit, packed on a whim. After smearing my chapped lips, I left the hotel and crossed the street to the beach, a slab of glistening polenta. With the conical roofs of the cabanas removed and resting like party hats on the sand, it was difficult to imagine that in season, this strip of sand leading to the swells of the Adriatic was filled with acres of bronzed and bikinied bodies.

As I picked up two or three shells, I felt Byron strolling beside me. Dragging his club foot, he confided the story about Lady Caroline Lamb who sent him her pubic hairs in a letter signed, "Your wild Antelope." And then the sound of hooves came roaring behind us and Byron left me to ride with his friend Shelley . . . *galloping over hillocks of shifting sand*. The shells in my hand still carried the scent of the sea creatures that once lived inside. I slipped them into my pocket.

When the afternoon grew unseasonably warm, I took a boat to Giudecca Island and the Cipriani, an isolated hotel with a saltwater pool, scheduled to close for the season. The landing place was marked by tall lapis-blue mooring posts with red and gold spires, poised like pens to write, at last, an autobiography of possibility.

I changed into my suit and entered the pool, where the reflection of San Giorgio's steeple shimmered on the water's surface like a diving board. I slid into the clear green water and, moving like a twenty-year-old, felt so glad to be alive, at that moment—*nel mezzo del cammin*—halfway down the road. Except that I saw my life not as a long walk, but as a long movie, and it was high time for intermission, a short break before the second part where I hoped everything would come together and propel the heroine toward a happy ending.

15

Quando l'amore non é pazzo, non é l'amore.
When love is not madness, it is not love.

From the top of Saint Mark's bell tower, two women leaned against the rail, surveying the city.

"Galileo demonstrated his telescope here," the short, dark-haired woman said.

"Must have been such a thrill to view the heavens close up for the first time," remarked her older companion, perhaps a sister. "And what was it he said about the sun? 'It ripens a bunch of grapes as though it had nothing else in the universe to do.'"

"Part of his argument about the infinite wisdom of the Divine, that the sun doesn't shine only for the grape—its rays affect a thousand other things."

The younger woman compared the scattered terra cotta rooftops to tiles from a casino board game. "A divine plan, or a game of chance?"

Together, the three of us turned our attention to the watercraft on the silvery lagoon. Legend has it that the gondola came from a fallen crescent moon, but the black boats moored in the water below reminded me of the way Bernie and I used to line up our slippers.

I thought of my parents, silver-haired sweethearts meant for each other, driving that morning to take me to lunch, harmonizing as they sang "Happy Birthday" into the phone and ending with "We love you!" And again, "We love you." Fainter, almost an echo that sounded more like "goodbye." When I spoke with the medical examiner, he said that they had died instantly and that when the bodies were recovered, they were holding hands.

What were the odds of meeting my soul mate on a raft of stone far, far from home? Listening for an answer, I heard only a rush of wind that sounded like the muffled echoes of dice boxes used long ago by casinos in the piazza. Then the Moors on the square's timepiece struck the hour, sending the pigeons into a cooing frenzy. The pair of bronze figures blackened by sea air bore the inscription *Horas non numero nisi serenas,* "I only count happy hours."

At the hotel, there was a message from Michael. It turned out that he, too, had reserved a room at the Gritti, and we arranged to meet at the bar that evening.

"Venice is great, but sometimes it doesn't feel real, with its tight quarters and time-warp," Michael said, after ordering our drinks.

"That's one of the things I love about it. It's a crucible, with all those lingering souls."

"I don't know about that . . . maybe it hasn't sunk in. I'm spending so much time with Benetton."

"How'd you happen to hook up with them?"

"I started as a student, modeling for them. They didn't care so much about my educational background or what field I was in. For them, image is key. They want people who project a present-tense image and products that send messages about social responsibility."

"And your favorites?"

"Sweaters are my mainstay, along with fragrances."

He held the back of his hand toward my nose. "And this one would be . . . ?"

"It's called 'Hot,'" Michael said. "And I brought along samples of our latest logos." He put his glass down and pulled a pair of emblems from his pocket. One patch read, "One Night Stand" and had a design of three arrows chasing each other in a circle. And the other, "Do It Smart," was superimposed on a heart.

"Not very romantic," I said, trying to imagine them in blue neon at the boat landings.

"Romantic?" He shrugged and stuffed them back in his pocket. "That's not the point—they're meant to be hip."

"And socially transforming?" I said.

"Hopefully." He flashed a smile.

Maybe I didn't have to fall head over heels. But sometimes, having been struck by the thunderbolt, it was a struggle to focus on Michael, when all I could really think about was Max.

"There's a market by Saint Thomas's Gate in Treviso where Benetton junkies flock for factory seconds at giveaway prices. Saturday mornings, if you ever want to go."

"Good to know. I can add it to my travelers' tips and I'll tell my friend Josie. She loves a bargain."

Michael wanted to know more about Josie, how we became friends, how long she was staying in Venice. Then he returned to shop talk.

"Over six thousand shops, in more than forty countries. With radio frequency identification, we can track our clothes worldwide."

"You don't remove them at the register?"

Michael shook his head. "Uh-uh. Saves a ton on inventory accuracy and theft management."

"You mean someone could drive by my house and know that I own a certain sweater?"

"Sure, but that's nothing to be ashamed of."

I took a sip of my wine.

"I'm going home in a couple of days, you know. I'm hoping we'll see each other when you get back to the States."

"Atlanta's a long way from Newburyport."

"Like you, Claire, I'm not afraid of traveling."

Michael could be sympathetic and understanding. He was a good-looking, sensible guy, but I felt I owed some allegiance to Max. After all, when I found myself discarded for a man, Max was the first to restore my sense of being a desirable woman.

"Michael, you've got a plane to catch in the morning. Why don't we call it a night?"

He left a generous tip, signing the credit card charge with a celebrity squiggle—the capital M legible—and then walked me to my door, gave me a kiss, and said, "I'll phone you when I get home."

In the morning, the desk attendant handed me a package wrapped in translucent paper and tied with a gauzy gold ribbon. A Loro Piana cashmere scarf, the size of a small blanket, with a palette of rose, ochre, and blue. It was soft in my hands, slipping from them like water. I draped it around my shoulders, and when I read the enclosed note, my heart skipped a beat.

"We'll always have Venice . . . Love, Max." As I slipped his note between the well-worn pages of my passport, I remembered the line from the final scene of *Casablanca*: *We'll always have Paris.* Rick to Ilsa, just before they part. Forever.

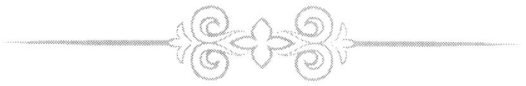

16

Fidarsi é bene, non fidarsi é meglio.
To trust is good; not to trust is better.

Josie was the only person on the planet who could get away with calling "Yoo-hoo!" from across the piazza. "No problem picking you out of the crowd," she said when we met halfway.

Unlike Marco Polo, I remained easily recognizable, at home and abroad. Inside, things were bubbling and shifting, but I dressed in the same old clothes and wore my hair in its predictable braid. Max's cashmere shawl was buried deep in my bag for safekeeping.

"Isn't this terrific?" Josie twirled, showing off her latest, a lambswool swing jacket. "I'm so glad I ran into you. Why don't you come for dinner? You can take a look at Ethan's watercolors—they're fantastic." Elbows hooked, we walked back to the ivy-covered house, Josie elaborating on the plans for her café back home.

"Hey, stranger." Ethan patted my shoulder, his hand encased in a yellow polka-dotted cooking mitt. Josie grated a block of parmigiano at the counter while Boccaccio strutted in his cage by the kitchen table.

"Ciao, Claire. Person-als," he croaked, cocking his head.

"Dinner's nearly ready," Ethan said. When he smiled, his eyes turned up at the corners as if they were smiling, too. "And be quiet, you," he added, waving his mitt toward the bird.

"What's he saying?" I asked.

"Oh, you know how he picks up phrases and shuffles them around," Ethan said, not answering my question. "Boccaccio—the nonsense that refreshes."

"Lately, he's been imitating that whistler at the boatyard," said Josie, leading me to the table where a blue McCoy vase of forsythia branches burst with yellow blossoms.

"And the ding of the microwave," said Ethan, arranging place settings for three.

"I swear he's as smart as any five-year-old," Josie said. "The parrot, that is." She grabbed Ethan and gave him a kiss. The three of us laughed, but I was feeling on edge ever since Boccaccio's greeting and his use of a word that sounded so much like "personals." I tried to make myself believe that this particular word had been stored in his walnut-sized hard drive since the day I'd first arrived, when Josie was pushing the idea of my advertising myself.

"C'mon," Josie said, continuing to the living room, "you've got to see these."

Watercolors in slim gold frames hung at eye level on all four walls. With limpid washes, Ethan had captured the evanescence of Venice.

"A lovely abstract quality," I said.

Josie and Ethan hugged and, cheek to cheek, danced a self-congratulatory tango. Then Josie broke away and led me to the side table to view her latest acquisitions.

"Isn't this sweet?" She held up a starched white apron, a handwritten recipe peeking from its pocket. "And how about this?" She waved a square of linen with one filet-crocheted corner that read in English, "Hot rolls make the . . ." On the opposite corner was a butterfly. She lined the basket with the vintage cloth, filled it with biscuits fresh from the oven, and set it on the table, along with the butter dish.

"Nice," I said.

Ethan carried a steaming platter to the table, penne cooked in vodka, heaped with fresh vegetables and a peppery cream sauce. As he decanted the Montepulciano, his reddish hair glowed golden in the candlelight and a harmonica winked from his shirt pocket.

"I've always thought of the harmonica as a mournful instrument," I said, seating myself. I looked around the table and wished that Max were sitting here with us.

"You can go either way with it, snappy tunes or melancholy ones. After dinner, I'll play a couple of Italian songs in your honor." He handed Josie and me our wine and poured mineral water for himself. "A toast," he said, raising his glass. "To friendship."

"To us," Josie said.

"*Cin, cin,*" I offered, as our three glasses gave a sharp, short ring. "Josie, where did you ever find forsythia this time of year?"

"In the courtyard. All it took was some warm water to make them think it's spring. Gardeners call it forcing, but I think of it as encouraging."

Throughout the meal, we shared stories about our various visits to the Guggenheim, the Accademia, and churches. I mentioned Mann's *Death in Venice*, Cornell's dream constructions, and the lonely Lido beach.

"You've been busy," Josie said. "I planned to get in touch if we didn't hear from you soon. We've been wanting to catch up."

"Besides getting to know Daniela and Nicole . . . remember, at the bridge? I've also met a couple of interesting guys."

"A *couple?*" Josie raised an eyebrow.

"I told you about Max, the art historian I met in the piazza." I took the shawl from my bag and draped it around my shoulders. "He gave me this."

"Looks expensive," Josie said. Ethan gave a low whistle.

"Then there's Michael, a businessman from Atlanta."

"Meeting Max first thing gave you time to get to know each other," Ethan said. "Josie's plan . . . " He put down his fork, adjusted his napkin.

"Plan?" I repeated.

"I mean Josephine," he glanced at Josie and continued, "planned this meal. Isn't it great?"

"I like just about anything Josie does," I said, triggering a long pause. "So, Ethan, you're from Maine?"

"Bainbridge Island, a short ferry ride from Seattle. But I traveled back East and poked around Monhegan, an island off the coast of Maine. That's where my mother's family comes from. Last summer, I stayed in the old homestead and folks were friendly toward me even though I was 'from away.'" He smiled at Josie. "Like the natives say, 'Nothing to do, but you get up early to do it.'"

He poured himself another glass of water. "Not like Bainbridge, which is real accessible, and more of a woodsy suburb. Monhegan's two miles of unspoiled quiet, a couple dozen art studios, a few pickups. The light's incredible, too, until the fog rolls in and confounds everything. And there's Cathedral Woods, just steps away from the surf, where little kids follow an island tradition of building fairy houses. When my mom and her brothers were young, they fashioned these tiny houses at the bases of trees, from bark and moss."

"That's so sweet," I said. "There's something about miniatures that makes us . . . ache."

"Ships in bottles," said Ethan.

"Lockets," Josie said, touching hers.

"Worlds within," I said.

"Anyway, I'm moving away from my gloomy, brooding mode," Ethan said. "Josie's helped me with that." Smiling at her, he described his strategy for assisting Josie at yard sales and flea markets, buying linens at the best price.

"You sound like a knight on a quest," I said.

"And we never use bleach. Learned that the hard way. Plain old sunshine and a bit of lemon juice will whiten them right up." I hoped for Josie's sake that he wasn't like Bernie who taught me how to remove chewing gum from the carpet, chocolate from my blouse, and my heart from my chest.

With a whoosh of wings, the African Grey flew into the dining room and landed on a forsythia branch.

"Boccaccio, watch out or you'll tip the whole damn thing over!" Josie scolded.

"Watch out!" the parrot echoed.

When he dropped to the tablecloth to peck at some remaining crumbs, I excused myself and headed for the bathroom. There, a tussie-mussie, the smallest of Victorian bouquets, was arranged in an old thimble on the sink. And what was this? On the shelf sat a jumbo-sized jar of Nutella, along with massage creams and perfumed oils. Curious, I opened the jar to find half the chocolate-hazelnut spread gone. With the door open a crack, I heard their voices from the kitchen.

"That was a close one," Josie was whispering. "You *cannot* mention the personal. It's bad enough that the bird brought it up."

That's when Boccaccio, on cue, screeched, "Match made in Heaven."

"Will you shut him up?" Josie said. I heard the cage door close and the sound of seeds being sprinkled on paper.

"I've got a problem keeping secrets," Ethan said. "Guess Boccaccio does, too." I heard a kiss.

I stared into the bathroom mirror and then, dipping my finger into the chocolate butter, wrote, "I know what you did." The kitchen grew quiet except for the clink of plates and glasses. The smeared mirror reflected the throbbing pale blue vein on my temple. My cheeks were on fire. Plan? Personal ad? My mind was racing. Realizing that I met Max because of Josie's interference made me sick to my stomach. I noticed the top button of my shirt hanging by one thread. I really was falling apart. I yanked it off, jammed it in my pocket, and returned to the conspirators in the kitchen.

"Josie, Ethan, dinner was really nice. It was great getting together, but I'm feeling tired. Hope you don't mind if I say goodnight." It took all the strength I had to deliver these lines without screaming, "What have you done? My trust in you and Max is all shot to hell!"

"Of course," Josie said, staring at me. Ethan wouldn't look at me and continued to scrub away at a pot.

Coming up behind him, I put my hand tentatively on his shoulder. "You won't mind if I catch your songs another time?"

He patted a soapy hand on my forearm, leaving a tiny hill of iridescent bubbles on my sleeve. Boccaccio dipped his bright red tail and cooed, "Ciao, Claire."

"Goodnight, all. And thanks again." I wanted to tell Josie that her lambswool coat was really creepy, with an off-putting texture that resembled the convoluted folds of her convoluted brain. Thoughts of the sunrise meeting at the piazza signaled a double betrayal—a close friend secretly running a personal ad and an art historian quietly playing along. Having a finger in the pie wasn't enough for Josie. She had to have *le mani in pasta*, both hands in the pasta.

After yet another email plea from my agent, I compromised on the communications issue and invested in a laptop because, although I continued to go cell-less, let's face it, I *am* a travel writer. I also arranged for an answering machine to be installed in my room. That evening, its light was blinking like a firefly in search of a mate. There were four messages: one from my agent, two from Bernie who had managed to track me down—It was important, he said. Whatever his problem, it could wait until morning—and the last message was from Michael, who said that things were going well in Atlanta, that he missed me, and that he couldn't wait to see me again. I reassessed my feelings toward Michael. I was really attracted to him and liked that our meeting had been authentic. We first spotted each other at the landing dock, an incident he didn't even remember! Then we met, again by chance, in the hotel lobby. Hugging my pillow, I fell asleep almost at once and dreamed I was up in the piazza's bell tower, staring at the heavens and at the ships at sea.

Having neglected to close the shutters, I awoke to a blast of sunlight and stumbled to the shower, relying on the steady spray of warm water to free up my thinking while I scribbled whatever words came to mind on the steamy glass door. This morning it was, "C-O-M-E," meaning to move toward something, to arrive. Or was it the Italian, *co-may*. How? Those rushed words whispered the night before—Josephine's plan, personals. The table had been set with flowers tricked into blooming when they should have remained dormant. Josie could work wonders, true. But she'd better not have forced anything in *my* life.

I phoned my agent.

"Page proofs are in the mail," she said. "Consider adding a few recipes. You know, for the kugeln, goulash. Readers like that sort of thing, even if they can't cook."

It was late morning by the time I tried to reach Bernie. His cell's voicemail was full, so I called Eric's place, where the machine picked up with some classical piece playing in the background and a lisping, "*Do* leave your name and number."

"It's Claire," I said. "I'll be in tonight, Bernie, if you want to give me a call."

Then I trudged over to Josie's place for coffee, and some words. I sat at her table while she ground the beans. Her hand was shaking, and Boccaccio was uncharacteristically quiet in his cage, as if he knew something was up.

"Josephine . . . "

She avoided my eyes.

"I forget—did you say you met Ethan through a personal?"

Her hand froze mid-air. "Don't you remember," she said, "we met at the auction, bidding on the same box of linens?"

"Right. You know, I could have sworn I overheard you mention something about a personal ad last night."

"I found your message in the bathroom." She pressed her lips together so hard they almost disappeared and took a pie from the refrigerator, a lime-colored glob oozing from under meringue. "I'm busted, okay? After you showed me your itinerary, I told him to be in the piazza at sunrise. And I gave him your whole schedule." She cut an over-generous slice and pushed it toward me.

"I'm not eating that." I imagined myself in a Three Stooges skit, tossing the pie in Josie's face. From there I could move on to a little eye gouging, shin kicking, and head knocking. Nyuk, nyuk.

"Claire . . . " Maybe like Larry the nebbish, she was about to say, "I'm sorry, Mo, it was all an accident."

"Josephine, how could you do that—without even asking my permission. I feel so *violated*. All this time I've been living with the fantasy that Fate brought Max and me together in the piazza. It was wildly romantic, kismet—just the two of us at sunrise, kissing a rose. And now I find out it wasn't Fate at all. You ran an ad, Max answered it, and I'm the foolish flower tricked into blooming out of season. Well, I'm pissed!"

"Maybe I should have told you."

"*Maybe*? Damn right you should have!" In a brief lapse, I reached for the fork.

"Remember that personal we worked on?" she said.

"*We*?"

"I liked that ad. I knew it would work."

"You really are shameless, aren't you? No boundaries whatsoever." I took a bite of pie.

"Twenty-seven responses, running only that one time." She looked positively triumphant. "They sent their replies to 'a travel writer's friend.' I had quite a job sorting through them, but there was this one. 'Down-to-earth, practical.' He said all the right things."

"Get to the point."

"He was made for you, an American who happened to be right here in Venice. You know how they say there's no such thing as coincidence? You *do* like him, don't you?" she asked, her voice turning giddy, her hands clasped as if in prayer.

"The age difference is one thing. But this . . . " I shook my head. "You've embarrassed me to death, depicting me as a desperate case, having to be advertised by my best friend. Max knew all about me ahead of time, and I didn't have a clue. He was even carrying my book with him, for goodness sake! And I fell for the whole thing."

Then it hit me. How when we first met, Max brought up the story about the chair at the Florian. He'd read the ad, answered it, and been handpicked by Josie as "the one." His expectations were high, really high, that he was meeting up with someone glamorous, intelligent, well traveled, fun. But when we came face-to-face, I was obviously older, stressing about the coffee cup, discouraging picnics, and all he could think of was that pathetic woman trying to steal the chair. So he came up with the story about an early appointment. Thunderbolt, my forty-five-year-old biscuits!

"Believe me, I didn't say anything to make you sound desperate, Claire."

"I haven't heard a word from him."

"He sent you that beautiful shawl."

"It was compensation."

"Compensation for what?"

My knees were shaking. I felt nauseous. "Maybe you meant well, but you didn't respect my wishes, and you know where the road of good intentions leads." Resorting to proverbs in conversation with my longtime friend was not a good sign. "This whole thing's a mess!"

Josie leaned toward me. "I'm sorry, Claire. You know I really care about you. And he seemed so right."

"I've got to go."

"Call me tonight?"

We'll always have Venice. That's what the note said. Signed, *Max.* Someone else might see the X at the end of his name as an exultant stick figure, or X-rated for our lovemaking, or X in a box that indicates a choice. But I was beginning to see it as an X to cross out a major mistake. I was deluged with X's: exile, exorcise, explore, express, exhale. Ex.

I was determined to put my life back in order. I could start with little things like replacing the shirt button that had fallen off at Josie's the other night. But the moment I settled into a soft chair with needle and thread, shirt and button, Bernie called.

"I'm excited about sharing some very special news with you." Deep breath, I told myself. "You're the first to hear it, with the exception of Eric, of course."

"Of course," I said, fingering the button.

"Well, it's our news really."

"*Really.*"

Visions popped up of Bernie and his newfound love dressed in tuxedoes, holding hands, a flower boy strewing rose petals, the organ playing some baroque music in an overly decorated church. "Don't tell me—you want me to be the matron-of-honor at your wedding."

"Better than that. We're going to have a baby."

"What in the world are you talking about, Bernie?"

"Eric and I. We each donated sperm to a surrogate mother that we chose to carry our child. We're sooo excited. We don't want to know whose sperm actually fertilized the egg, Eric's or mine, because we both want to feel totally invested." The pounding in my ears kept me from hearing another word until, "Claire, we'd be honored."

"What?"

"I thought this would help mend bridges, bring us together again in friendship. We'd be honored if you'd agree to be the baby's godmother."

"You mean *fairy* godmother?" I clasped my hand over my mouth.

A somewhat forced laugh. "Okay, right—fairy godmother."

My sobbing started slowly, silently, an awkward wracking and heaving of my entire body. I shook my head from side to side. "No, no, no. I can't believe you're doing this. You know how much I wanted a baby and now . . . "

"And now," said Bernie, "You'll be a part of this baby's life. It would fill that gap for you."

"I am so sick of having people around me decide what's best for me, what will make me happy—what I need!"

"Maybe it's time you stopped moping."

"And what would you know about moping?" I accidentally jabbed my finger with the needle and yelled out in pain.

"What's wrong?"

"I just stabbed myself."

"Oh, Claire."

"With *a sewing needle*, Bernie." I blew my nose loudly and watched a little red globe form on my fingertip.

Bernie cleared his throat. More silence. "I never told you this . . . " More throat clearing. "But as a kid I loved to hang around my mother while she ironed." His voice shifted to a monotone. "I know it sounds strange, but I got high on the smell of steam and clean clothes. I replaced missing buttons for her. Double threaded the needle, tied the knot. That was easy. But the actual sewing on of the button was always tricky. Pushing the needle up through the hole. I kept hitting the back of the button, poking around for a place to push the needle through."

"So what's all this *crap* about buttons?" I said, my voice shrill.

"When I turned nine, something happened, smooth and quick. No more hit or miss, no more poking around with the needle and thread. I could sew those buttons on without a hitch, because once I stopped trying so hard, it was easy. About that time, I knew I was attracted to boys, but I was afraid to be different, to follow those instincts. I forced myself to fit into the dating scene, and marriage. Well, of course, you know about that stage of my life."

"Of course," I said. "It's always about *your* life. Did you ever, ever think about anyone but yourself?"

"Eric thought that you . . . "

"Bernie, shut the hell up."

I slammed the phone down and took a hot bath, adding my tears to the soapy water. Then I curled up in bed with an extra comforter and turned on the TV. But I couldn't get all the baby showers I had attended over the years off my mind, all those heartbreaking favors, the pink and blue plastic cradles, smiling storks and pastel mints. Damn!

When the phone rang, I let the machine pick up. It was a message from Josie about her yoga class. Then Max left his number and asked me to call back. I didn't want to play phone tag, or musical chairs, for that matter. I closed my eyes and pictured the chairs at the Florian. When the music stopped, I'd be the one left standing, alone. My indignation sparked, igniting memories of my first, sweet lovemaking with Max. I couldn't trust my best friend, and I no longer believed in love-at-first-sight. Part of me said, so what? But another, larger part of me felt tricked and deceived.

Mozartkugeln
(Josie calls them "Mozart Balls")

1 cup hazelnut nougat
1 1/2 cups marzipan
1/3 cup confectioners' sugar
A shot of kirsch
1/4 cup pistachios
3/4 cup milk chocolate coating
3/4 cup dark chocolate coating

Form three dozen little balls with the nougat.
Mix the marzipan, sugar, kirsch, and the crushed pistachios, reserving some nuts for decoration.
Form a long roll of dough and cut into 36 pieces.
Coat each nougat ball with a layer of marzipan mix and set aside.
Melt the milk chocolate.
Place each ball on a bamboo skewer and dunk in chocolate. Place stick vertically with ball at the top on a platform. Allow chocolate to harden. Then melt dark chocolate and cover each ball with a thin layer using the same method. Sprinkle with reserved pistachios. Remove stick and fill hole with chocolate coating.

Be sure to have a secret hiding place.

17

Meglio un uovo oggi che una gallina domani.
Better an egg today than a chicken tomorrow.

I ignored Max's call. I wanted him to suffer. And I wanted to suffer, too, so when I saw the marquee at the Accademia Theater advertising *Death in Venice*, I bought a ticket and took an aisle seat down front. During the commercials and coming attractions, I imagined glancing over at Max's profile in the dim light, wishing that with a simple turn of the head, I could count on that same profile over the years. But the seat beside me remained empty.

I'd seen this film based on Thomas Mann's novella ages ago and remembered it as dark with almost no dialogue. Dirk Bogarde plays Gustav, his lined face reflecting a lifelong quest for perfection that seemed to droop with the sheer weight of the soundtrack, Mahler's Fifth.

Bogarde kept his homosexuality under wraps, like you-know-who had up until you-know-when, but the upside was that being a repressed homosexual probably helped Bogarde play a repressed homosexual. I felt such compassion for him, a Jew who served in the British army, devastated by what he witnessed at Bergen-Belsen.

I scrunched down in my seat to witness Gustav's last days in Venice skulking in shadowy alleyways, traipsing after an androgynous Polish boy, the unattainable Tadzio. It was all dark and disturbing, and difficult to grasp the complexity of Gustav's struggle. The film felt embalmed, and the Hôtel des Bains rested like an old cake covered in marzipan, something like Miss Havisham's ruined mansion.

I couldn't take any more, spotted the Massinis cuddled together in a back row as I left, and was out the door before the fresh dye applied to Gustav's hair turned watery in the heat and trickled in inky rivulets down his sweaty temples. I made my way down the alley as Gustav languished in his beach lounge, near death, his arm outstretched toward Tadzio's beckoning silhouette on the horizon. And by the time Gustav clasped his hand over his heart and stopped breathing, I was strolling along the Canal.

I found a bench and sat to contemplate the water traffic. It was then that, like a polite guest, Thomas Mann's shade appeared, a Panama hat shielding his eyes and hiding most of his salt-and-pepper hair. The writer wore crisp linen pants and a button-down vest that looked like new, but emitted an odor of mothballs. Herr Mann brushed a piece of lint from his lapel and considered me from behind wire-rimmed spectacles. Then he leaned forward, his mustache close enough to tickle my ear. When he spoke, his tone was confidential. "Chance encounters, countless close-knit possibilities," he whispered. In the next moment, he faded away with faint fumes of naphthalene.

In the story, Gustav pursued an impossible love interest, sacrificed his self-respect, and in the end, lost everything. And all the while he tried to bolster himself with the phrase that Mann repeated to me. "Countless possibilities . . ."

A week later Michael, back in town, gave me a call. "How've you been?"

"A change of pace would do wonders," I told him.

After feeding the pigeons in Saint Mark's, we explored a maze of ancient alleys, coming across the unexpected sight of a pineapple resting on one of the doorsteps.

"A sign of hospitality," I said. "Used by sea captains to signal their return from exotic places. Never seen it here in Venice."

"Common in the Northeast, isn't it, with all those whaling captains?"

"Like lions in Venice, they're everywhere."

A woman came down the stairs, collected the fruit, and went back inside.

"So much for that welcome mat," I said, laughing.

"I didn't exactly have the welcome mat out when you and I first met," Michael said, "I talked about my dead relationship, sounded bitter about my divorce. I guess I . . ."

"I understand, believe me. It's something you need to get through. There's an antique house near Newburyport with a whole corner missing because, the story goes, the road was too narrow for Lafayette's coach to pass, so the owner hacked off part of his home to make way. After Bernie and I split, I felt like that funny-looking house, a big chunk of me missing, destroyed to clear the path for someone else's happiness. I think the one who leaves is always better off, don't you?"

"Only if we let them. And listen to yourself, describing those feelings in the past tense. All we need to do is banish the ghosts from our love life."

Banish them from our *lives*, period. Michael took my hand, raised it to his lips, and kissed my fingertips. Then he hooked his arm through mine as we searched for a *trattoria*. "I'm sorry that last time we saw each other, I got caught up in discussing my work. That's another habit of mine that's hard to break." We sat at a table covered with a red and white checked cloth and ordered big bowls of minestrone. After our meal, Michael led me to a courtyard where a group of evergreens stood like guardians, and I thought of Max, how he smelled of the forest. I once thought of Max as my cathedral of pines where, instead of fairy houses, I constructed fragile hopes and daring dreams. I thought there might still be hope.

When Michael and I settled in on a bench, I told him about Bernie and Eric and how they were expecting a baby.

"I've always wanted kids," Michael said. "At the bookstore, I find myself wandering to the parenting section to thumb through the new titles or eavesdropping during story hour in the kiddy section. Anyway, the good thing about your ex being gay is that you know there's no possibility for reconciliation. That door's closed. There's no other woman to bruise your ego, and none of what happened was your fault. It wasn't anyone's fault. In a way, I envy you."

That night I tossed and turned, filled with a restless energy. I remembered how gentle Michael's mouth felt on my fingers. My fondness for him was growing, and I was beginning to treasure our time together. I remembered a remark that Ethan had made while working on one of his paintings, trying to generate enough pieces to have a one-man show. "When the time comes, I won't worry about critics. The artist swims in the water, while the critic stands ashore. I *like* being in the water." I needed to stop being fearful and get in the water. Isn't that what the *Madonna of the Vegetable Patch* advised? I must fill my heart with love and "take the plunge."

Ethan, Josie, Michael, and Max were all champion swimmers in the Grand Canal of life. But I felt like a hesitant bystander waiting on the banks like a figure in Giorgione's *Tempest*—watching, weighing my options.

When I tired of surfing the Net for chocolate kugeln recipes, I picked up some fried seafood to take back to my hotel room where I watched a little TV. But I could only put up with so many mattress ads, their models always in pairs—dancers with arms reaching, those who snuggled, those who hugged, and those who slept bum to bum. Those ads never show anyone in bed alone.

In the morning, I was sick to my stomach. It may have been the seafood, but I chalked it up to nerves. I took a shower, dressed, and went to Josie's place. She made me a cappuccino, and the soothing smell of cinnamon calmed me.

"Forgiven me yet?" she said.

"You and Max, you mean." It was puzzling that Max continued to keep the personal ad a secret. Then I remembered how threatened I felt when I saw him alone with Isabella and reminded myself that there was a lot about Max that I didn't know.

Josie wrapped some ice in a dishtowel and handed it to me. "Here. Your eyes are all puffy."

"I've got some news." Holding the towel against my face, I delivered my line. "Bernie is having a baby."

Josie's mouth fell open. "I can't believe it!"

"I know. He's full of surprises, isn't he?"

"And what about Max. Have you heard from him?"

I averted my eyes and mumbled, "Not exactly."

"What does *that* mean?" she said, lips pursed, hand on hip.

"He left his number."

"So you *have* heard from him. This could all be very simple, if you'd . . . "

"Josie, I don't want any more advice!" I slammed the cloth down. Cubes of melting ice scattered across the table. I felt as Hepburn's character must have felt in *Summertime*, when her dignity dropped to the floor with her dress.

Josie took a paper bag from the cupboard and pushed it in my direction. "I picked up this spice rack for you. See? Capped bottles, like Cornell's. Now you can make a pharmacy of your own."

"It's going to take more than a bunch of old bottles to fix this, Josie. I'm still furious with you."

"Claire, I was wrong to run that ad. I'm *really, really,* sorry." She took a minute to wring out the soggy cloth and wiped down the counter. "Come with me tonight to yoga class? I could use the moral support."

Back in my room, I rifled through my pockets and found a feather from Saint Mark's, shells from the Lido, and a boat ticket to Burano, to slip into the bottles. Grieg's "Lonely Pilgrim" was playing on the radio. I felt like a pilgrim who might never arrive, forever postponing happiness. I needed to take a good look at where I was going and forget about the roads traveled, the time passed. Changing houses or partners was one thing, but changing my restless self was another. Hadn't Proust hinted about this when he advised me to gain new eyes? I curled up in bed and took a long nap.

The yoga teacher, Chantal, assumed the lotus position, inviting us to do the same. She assured us that there was no need to be judgmental, that we were there to be kind to ourselves. But my knees creaked, and my anklebones pressed painfully against the hardwood floor through the thin mat. Keep our spines straight and imagine light filtering through the tops of our heads, she said. But when I grasped my knees and tried to straighten my back, my ligaments twisted and several vertebrae cracked.

"I've brought each of you a present," Chantal crooned, handing out neckties from a basket. Mine was decorated with a constellation of coffee stains. She directed us to lie flat on our backs, loop the tie under the soles of both feet and pull on the ends to stretch the leg muscles.

"No white knuckles!" Chantal called out like a drill instructor. "White knuckles mean stress."

Demons were rampaging through my body, deconstructing my whole physical being. We moved from one posture to another, all impossible: the Warrior, some hip-twisting contortion, then the Cobra, which felt as if two cobras had me in their fangs and were pulling me apart. At one point, a frowning Chantal studied me while I groaned and grunted. "Are you okay?" she mouthed.

I nodded, but remained in perpetual pain until we reached the Child position. The Table was better, but the Corpse was my all-time favorite. I just lay on my back and breathed deeply, in through the nose, out through the mouth. I heard Chantal say something about taking responsibility, getting beyond the ego, how the soul awaits those who travel its path. For the hour and a half of yoga, I worried about nothing, except whether I'd ever walk again. I limped home, but didn't admit to Josie that I felt lighter. I wasn't about to leave myself open to any remarks such as, "See? I know what's good for you."

I crawled into bed and thumbed through my latest purchase, a book on Cornell. "Haunting best describes his hotel boxes," the author wrote, referring to the artist's miniature lobbies of Parisian hotels, because "each of us is a transient." Rooms at the Accademia, La Calcina, Max's apartment, the Londra, and the Gritti were all rented rooms with beds slept in by a string of lovers all headed for the final destination.

Aware of a peculiar sound, something like a weary wheeze, coming from the television set, I closed the book and stared at the blank screen. At first, like a convex mirror, it encompassed only a reflection of the room's contents, but incrementally, a foggy figure curled in on itself, then opened, stretched, and gathered into the form of a man in gray pants and an oxford shirt, worn at the collar. Joseph Cornell emerged from the screen and came to sit on my bed as if it were the most natural thing in the world. He removed his scuffed shoes and emptied the contents of his pockets, placing them on the nightstand as precisely as I arrange my own things on any hotel dresser: a bottle cork, a cordial glass, a child's block, a celestial map. Then he stretched out on the comforter beside me and rested his hand on my tummy.

When the phone rang, I let the answering machine pick up. No message.

"You must start taking your calls, Claire," he murmured. "You really must." I couldn't take my eyes off his feet. Cornell's socks were brown with red heels and red toes, the kind used to make old-fashioned monkey dolls.

"Life is full of delights," he said. I nestled my head against his shoulder and dreamed of sailing to the Lido, a baby in my arms.

In the morning, Josie invited me over for a cappuccino. "You're green around the gills," she said, staring at me over the rim of her mug.

"I don't feel so great." My stomach churned at the sight of the croissants, and I could barely touch my warm, frothy drink. I was still hoping against hope that Josie would lean across the table and say, "You know what? I never ran any personal ad, you silly. It was all a practical joke."

"Will you come to the auction in Mestre with me tonight?"

"Don't think I can," I said. "I must've picked up a bug."

"All those boat rides in the cold and damp. Go back to your hotel and take a nap. I'll stop by at six to check on you."

Bundled up in bed, with the TV on mute, I called Max's number. It was great to hear his voice on the recording: "Hey there, this is Max. Leave a message, I'm all ears." I could have said, "I love your ears and the rest of you, too. Sorry I haven't called sooner. I hope your mother's feeling better and that we can talk soon." But I didn't say any of that. I hung up.

That afternoon a package arrived in the mail, a framed photo of me with the stack of Florian chairs in the background.

"For your friend," the note read. I ached to fall again into his arms, to float in our night of love and *acqua alta*. But more than anything, I wanted to work up the courage to overcome my injured pride and confront him about the personal ad.

At six, Josie came by and dragged me out of bed. Faulty fluorescent lights in the packed auction hall created a dizzying strobe effect that, combined with the mustiness of vintage goods, challenged the shaky status of my digestive system. I reached for my box of saltines.

"Glad you're feeling better," Josie said, intent on the items for sale and oblivious to my discomfort. "Probably one of those twenty-four-hour things." In minutes, she successfully bid on three boxes of linens.

"Is this where you and Ethan met?"

"He sat right there in that folding chair." She pointed to the seat where a white-haired woman looking like Mother Time cradled an antique clock. "He's finally able to put together a one-man show in Treviso, and I'm catering the opening," she said, going through one of the boxes. "I'd love it if you'd help me."

"I'll think about it."

"Would you take a look at the embroidered yoke on this little cotton dress?" she squealed.

I finished the whole box of saltines in no time.

18

Se sono rose, fiorianno.
If they are roses, they will bloom.

It became impossible to hold anything down. And my breasts felt as if someone had spent the night pummeling them. Uh, oh. In seconds, I was online at a site called R-U-Pregnant.com, staring at a photo of an expectant mother with her hand on her belly. And guess what? Some women experienced nausea within weeks, even days of conception.

In my bathroom, I read the directions on the box twice, imagining the millions of women around the globe who had gone through this same ritual. My hand shook as I checked the strip, and when I saw that it was a two-striper, my heart felt as if it would pound right out of my chest. What did the instruction sheet say, again? My hand was shaking so much I could barely read the print. One colored band, no. Two colored bands . . . I am pregnant. Pregnant! PREGNANT! Expecting. In the family way, with child. It's what I've always wanted.

About to faint, I rested against the toilet tank, then put my spinning head between my knees. Everything turned black. Moments later, blood returned to my head, saliva to my mouth. I couldn't possibly have a baby. I couldn't possibly give it up. A baby. *Bimba al bordo.* The phrase trumpeted in my ear. Rising in slow motion, I wandered around the room, touched the backs of chairs, straightened the carpet with the toe of my shoe, and danced back and forth at each window, patting my flat belly. My world had changed. I was seeing everything for the first time.

I created a new file, a Pregnancy To-Do list that I downloaded from R-U-Pregnant. To ease nausea, wristbands that put gentle acupressure on the sixth meridian point were suggested. I was map reading again, but this time the foreign country was my body and nei-kuan was a prime location.

Getting in touch with Max seemed ridiculous now, but it was the only thing to do. And say what? "Hey, remember me? I'm pregnant." My head continued to spin. It would help if I had someone to talk to. In the past, Josie would have been the first to know, but I couldn't risk sharing the news with her. Bernie, no way. Daniela? She was in the city, I remembered. I called and asked if we could meet.

Something deep inside was bubbling, something irrepressible that refused to be pushed down. I would eat more sensibly and get out of bed slowly. I imagined a new book on the horizon—*Baby on Board*. I imagined a chorus of babies screaming in agony on planes because their little Eustachian tubes couldn't handle the fluctuating air pressure. I imagined toting a Snugli into foreign restaurants, always on the go—trains, buses, cars, boats, and planes. It wouldn't do. No, no, no. I walked around in a trance, repeating, "I've got time to think this through. I have time."

Daniela hugged me when we met, and I told her my news. "Are you happy about this, Claire?"

"I, I . . . yes."

"Then it will all work out, *cara.*"

We spent the afternoon going in and out of shops, including a bookstore where she showed me a memoir about a man who spots a woman at the Florian and falls head-over-heels for her.

"It reads like a fable. And an interesting parallel to your own experience, no?" Daniela said. "These two marry and spend their days cooking eel in bay leaves, sardines in onion marinade, crispy apple and pine nut fritters."

"Sounds delicious," a familiar voice piped up.

"Chef Nicolò," I said, turning. His silvery hair, free of the tall white hat, fell in thick stylish waves against the collar of his dark suit. His eyes were fixed on Daniela.

"*Piacere. Molto piacere,*" he said, with some reverence when I made introductions. "An honor to meet you. And may I say, you are welcome to visit my kitchen anytime. I'm sure we have much to share."

"That would be delightful," Daniela said, her dancing eyes straying to his ring-less hand.

The weekend before Thanksgiving, Josie and I drove a rented car to Treviso for Ethan's opening. It was a great escape, and as each mile passed, I felt more excited about the baby and less angry about Josie's interference. I had been to the doctor's, taken tests, and was pronounced disease-free, so I was worry-free. Pretty much, anyway. And if I ever spoke with Max again, I would tell him to cross STD's off *his* worry list, if he had one.

"Ethan had a tough childhood and fell in with a bad crowd," she said, eyes fixed on the road.

"Oh?" I fished in my bag for a mint.

"He was arrested on a DUI. That's why he left Seattle." She glanced over at me.

"I see." I unwrapped my candy, offering her one.

"He swears he's been clean for a year now."

"Still, don't you think you should be careful?" Pot and kettle.

She shook her head. "I've *been* careful and where's it gotten me? Playing pastry chef back home at the Buoy-oh-Buoy. Selling linens on eBay. Rehabbing my house. And let's not forget Beau and Nick."

How could I forget Beau and Nick? Beau was a creative guy loaded with charm who couldn't hold down a job. He got drunk at a relative's wedding, and later that night at Josie's parents' home, stripped off all his clothes and ran around the house naked. Her father got so pissed off that he chased Beau out of the house with a shotgun. Nick was a self-employed control freak. "Exceedingly frugal" is how Josie described him. I saw him as amazingly cheap, a subscriber to *Tightwaddery Gazette* who got excited about the concept of earwax as an alternative to lip balm. He used stray hairs to clean between his teeth to save on dental floss, for goodness sake.

"As funny and full of life as you are, Josie, maybe you just haven't found the right guy."

"Ethan is right for me."

"Could we stop for a minute?"

"Sick again?"

"Look at those clouds," I said, admiring them through the windshield. "Wisps of cotton candy."

"What's going on with you, Claire? You've been in a funk for days, and suddenly you're so damned upbeat!"

Josie pulled over and stopped the car. I got out and danced around, gulping deep breaths of fresh air.

"Okay. You're going to tell me what's up," she said when I climbed back in.

"We'll talk about it later."

"When, later?" She bit a glossy fingernail.

"On the way home."

"Grrr. This is going to drive me crazy!"

In Treviso, I made the coffee while Josie set the table with her prize linens, saying, "These will look great in my café, don't you think?"

Ethan checked and double-checked his artwork, making sure the prices were right and the watercolors were properly hung.

By eight o'clock the place was packed. People scoffed down Josie's artfully constructed *cichetti*, and red "sold" stickers popped up in the corners of the paintings. By nine-thirty, only one piece remained unsold, a scene in the Grand Canal, a gondolier teaching his young son how to use an oar. I placed a sticker on it and claimed it for myself.

On the way home, I broke the news to Josie.

"I can't believe it!" The car veered dangerously. "How did that happen? You didn't use protection?"

"Honestly, I didn't think much about it." I remembered Max coming to my bed in the pitch black, kissing my ear, whispering sweet nothings about Ruskin and Venetian architecture, but I wasn't going to go into any more detail with my friend about how *It Happened One Night*.

"When are you planning to tell . . . " she stopped. "It is Max, isn't it?"

"Of course, it's Max!" I snapped.

Josie didn't offer any personal advice. Instead, she gushed about choosing a name, the benefits of breastfeeding, and how and where to locate premium vintage baby clothes and pillowcases, while I hoped silently that the baby would, with any luck, inherit my mom's delectable dimples, my dad's endearing cowlick, Max's deep brown eyes.

"This calls for a celebration," Josie said, parking in front of a candy shop. "I'll be right out." I sat in the car while she ran in and soon emerged with a large box of Baci chocolates. We left the car in Piazzale Roma and walked to my hotel room, where she broke open the box and handed me a candy covered in star-studded foil. When I unwrapped it, an enclosed slip of paper dropped to the floor. She picked up the fortune and read it to me. "Everything you ever wanted is right at your fingertips. All you have to do is reach out." I could tell she was making it up as she went along.

She flinched when she heard the edge to my voice. "Stay out of this. You need to promise you won't interfere. Because it's *my* life! I have strong feelings for Max, but I'm not rushing into anything, especially now."

"Okay, okay," she said, eyeing the candy.

"Max is younger and impulsive. I don't know whether he's ready for this kind of commitment."

"Alright, already. I understand. You have to weigh your options."

I offered her a chocolate for positive reinforcement. It was time to prepare for a new life, starting now, a life with my baby. I reached for a candy, peeled the wrapper, and read the strip of paper inside. *Soli siamo incompleti . . . .* We're incomplete alone; that's why we seek a kindred spirit. After Josie left, I slipped the message into one of my pharmacy bottles. A kindred spirit is someone who shares the same beliefs, attitudes, and feelings. I wondered who my kindred spirit might be.

Sleep was out of the question, so I watched *Cinema Paradiso* for the umpteenth time. At his mentor's funeral, Salvatore inherited a montage, a reel of passionate kisses censored by the village priest and rescued by the projectionist. This got me thinking about what we save and what we throw away. I felt sorry for Salvatore, whose love life was nonexistent. I vowed not to end up like him, or like the Florian chair lady.

I reached for another candy. "Limited love is never real love," the note cautioned. What could be sadder than looking back on a life filled with regret? There was no answer when I phoned Max again, so I left a message. Hours later, when he didn't call back, I wondered whether he'd given up on me. Oh well, maybe it was all for the best, I rationalized. But I cried myself to sleep that night.

The beginning of the week went by in a blur. Josie's dozen guests gathered around her Thanksgiving table—"What a wonderful tradition these Americans have!" one of them said—a gracious Ethan, several neighbors, student chefs and their spouses, as eclectic a mix as Josie's mismatched place settings. For the occasion, her blue vase held a tangle of woody vines, orange berries encased in open yellow capsules. Bittersweet.

Dinner conversation centered on topics of market freshness, seductive simplicity, the joys of seasonal food. Along with goose, we feasted on specialties such as ravioli Marco Polo, homemade pasta stuffed with tuna and ginger, and a rich risotto of wild mushrooms and truffle oil.

"*Baccalà,* salt cod, was introduced by Bartolomeo Scappi," one of the guests said.

"I'd like to get my hands on a copy of *his* cookbook," another said. "The Pope's personal chef, wasn't he?"

"In the 1500s."

"Probably includes bizarre dishes like flambéed flamingo tongues."

"You're thinking of the ancient Romans. And they were boiled. Please."

Another student described the Neapolitan way to prepare a peacock. "You skin it from breast to tail, baste it with grease, stick it with whole cloves. Then it's stuffed, cooked, and redressed in its own skin, which has been coated with spices, *un pizzico di sale*, a pinch of salt, and cinnamon. Give it iron legs on which to stand so that it seems alive. A little camphor on cotton in the beak, soaked in old wine, set on fire and it will breathe flames for a long time. A dish to suit the Marchesa Casati."

While Ethan entertained the guests, I joined Josie in the kitchen to pack up the leftovers. Picking the carcass clean, she set the wishbone on the windowsill. I didn't even know at this point what I wished for, other than a healthy baby. Everything else fell by the wayside.

Josie wiped her hands on a towel, took several champagne flutes from the freezer, and said over her shoulder, "Ask how many would like a peacock, please?"

"Didn't we just have a goose?"

"Oh, you're such a kidder!" She poured green Chartreuse in each frosted glass, added crushed ice, then a layer of semi-frozen grenadine. When I returned with a count of eight, she was scooping lemon sherbet.

"Here, sprinkle some Strega on this, will you?" she said, handing me the bottle of liqueur. "And a peacock in a pear tree," she sang, as she garnished each drink with a single mint leaf and a cherry.

Later that evening, I got a call from Michael. "I'm helping out at the megastore in Rome. Would you be willing to come down? This place is going to be humming by five a.m. Hundreds of customers camped out with sleeping bags. We're offering free gift wrapping, and I'm not very good at that sort of thing. I'll make it worth your while. Just for a couple of days. What do you say?"

This was a pretext because Michael must have a dozen employees able to wrap packages. But the day after Thanksgiving was a guaranteed letdown, so I began throwing things into my bag before we even said goodbye.

Lining Rome's Via Corsi—a street once used by Pope Paul II for horse races—are palaces, churches, and shops. The Benetton store takes up three floors of an eighteenth-century building and offers a full range of products, including a hairdressing service for children.

Michael stood behind a counter stocked with large rolls of decorative paper on metal dispensers and a variety of curling ribbon and satiny adhesive tape. I wondered whether his night table held a dog-eared handbook with a special section entitled, "Make yourself irresistible: Ask for help." It didn't matter. This was bound to be more fun than sitting alone in my hotel room.

I waded through wall-to-wall customers and handed Michael a box of baked goods from Josie, who was asking a lot of questions about him lately.

"If I didn't know better, I'd say you were interested in him for yourself," I told her.

"I'm looking out for your best interests, that's all."

When I said, "Not your job, Josie," she opened her mouth and closed it without saying another word.

Once the registers opened, customers lined up with arms full of sweaters, each to be individually wrapped. I followed the example of the signora at the Boscolo bakery and took care to make each package special.

"You're terrific, you know that?" Michael said at the end of the day.

I admired him as we sat across the table from each other at dinner that evening. Michael would never detach a statue's private parts, flail his arms at the risk of endangering fellow diners, present a date with wilted roses, or overlook the need for a condom. And no way would he consider balancing a cup on one knee.

"Michael, I need to tell you something." I waited for his blue-gray eyes to meet mine and fought an unexpected urge to get up and take his face in my hands. "I need to tell you that I've been seeing someone." I stopped short of telling him about the pregnancy.

"I thought that might be the case." His voice dropped. "I can't pretend I'm not hurt. And disappointed." Michael reached across the table and took my hand. "I like you, Claire. A lot. Maybe we can keep this, I don't know, kind of fluid?"

"I'm not sure about this other relationship, but I do want to see where it goes."

"Still, I'd like to stay in touch."

"We'll see," I said. And we left it at that.

I slept on his sofa, but tossed and turned all night long. Part of me wanted to get up and slip into bed with him, cuddle up and lure him in with seductive talk about . . . Benetton sweaters: the knit and purl, the color and texture, the basket-weave, the cable. He was so easygoing, so understanding. Maybe I would tell him about the pregnancy and maybe not. He would never have to know that Max was the father. But wasn't I the one committed to truth and authenticity? Still, his closed bedroom door seemed to beckon to me. All I had to do was get up, take a dozen steps, turn the handle, and the rest would be so easy. But I remained on the sofa.

In the morning, I was thrilled when he presented me with a stack of boxes.

"Some must-haves," he said. I squealed over jewel colors of teal, claret, and pink. I oohed and aahed over the pale blue and mauve of Paris in a fleecy angora blend; a pullover with broad, horizontal stripes of bright royal blue, shocking pink, and turquoise; and a knitted coat that brushed the ground like a queen's train.

"I'll miss you," Michael said, as I modeled one of the new sweaters. I was warmed by a rare feeling of being cared for, in a familiar way, like my parents had cared for me. When he embraced me, I lay my head on Michael's shoulder longer than either of us expected and was sorry when he let me go.

Before catching the train to Venice, I spent time at the Borghese Gallery viewing a Madonna credited to Raphael's prodigy, Giulio Romano. It reminded me of one I'd seen in Milan where Raphael portrayed a tranquil Joseph and Mary taking their vows while another man, angered at his failure to win Mary, breaks a stick over his knee. I pictured Michael and Max but wasn't sure who might fit the role of Joseph and who the angry suitor.

19

Troppi cuochi guastano la cucina.
Too many cooks spoil the kitchen.

"I'm going to pick up some bread. Be right back," Josie said, leaving me alone with Ethan, who was scoring peeled cucumbers with a fork to create a decorative edge, before cutting them into thin slices.

"She told you some of my history," he said.

"Well, you shouldn't worry. What's past is past," I said, chopping the carrots.

"Alcohol's a dead end, I know that. There are times I'd sell my soul for a drink. But the point is, I don't do it. It's been more than a year since I've touched a drop. Josie's my high now—Josie and my art. They're more than enough." He sliced tomatoes while I rinsed and dried the arugula.

"I appreciate your bringing it up," I said as he tossed the salad makings in a wooden bowl. I took the plate of tuna from the fridge, noticed the empty cage by the window. "Where's Boccaccio?"

"Oh, he's taken to hanging out in the bedroom," Ethan said. "He's hooked on the nature channel." After setting the table, I went in to say hello, but Boccaccio was intent on watching a program about parrots in southern Asia that sleep upside down. On the table beside him, three waxy berries, like baby teeth, had fallen from the mistletoe and lay beside a potted Christmas cactus bursting with pink blossoms, right on schedule. To everything there is a season. But I was in the wrong season, pregnant at forty-five.

Walking back to the hotel after dinner, I noticed that signs of the season had sprung up everywhere—mooring posts topped with Santa hats, stone lions sprouting fluffy white beards, and tiny fairy lights twinkling in window boxes. I held my breath at the sight of eight red-suited, overstuffed Santas attempting to board a gondola to some unknown destination.

A cutaway chambered nautilus on the table in the waiting room of the doctor's office reminded me of *The French Lieutenant's Woman* and the author's comment that a woman's mind is as convoluted as the nautilus. In the story, the couple falls in love under false pretenses. The woman, Sarah, fabricates an air of mystery, pretending to be the French lieutenant's mistress in order to win over a lover. But the relationship is based on a lie, and when she becomes pregnant, their love is doomed.

In the end, Sarah, an avid follower of Ruskin's theories on false origins, ditches her lover in order to set things straight. I could relate to Sarah because once I learned about the personal ad and the arranged meeting, everything I had with Max felt counterfeit. How could I be sure that he loved me for myself?

Each year the nautilus abandons its dwelling chamber for a new one. I still had a chance, or maybe more than a single chance, for love. Life was generous, and I need not limit myself to one particular destiny when I could help myself to a bowlful of Baci, each with its own fortune.

"As soon as I get back to Newburyport, I'm opening that coffee shop. Ethan is very enthusiastic about it." Josie's eyes were sparkling.

"I've had my fill of islands," Ethan said. "I'm looking forward to some mainland living."

"And I got this idea from a magazine for three-dimensional photos of the dessert choices. Ethan is taking the pictures. Customers wear 3-D glasses to read the menu. What do you think?"

"I don't know," I said, studying my hands.

She took a closer look at me. "Are you okay?"

I bit my lip. "There's something so phony about how Max and I met. I can't seem to get beyond that."

"Oh, Claire, don't worry about it. Look at it as the hand of Fate." Josie smiled. "Or divine intervention."

"Well, well," said Ethan. "Doesn't my little love have a big head?"

When Max called, my heart leaped despite my reservations. "I have something to tell you," he said. "I hate doing it over the phone, but . . . "

This was it! A declaration of love, a promise of commitment, or possibly a proposal of marriage. "Yes?" I held my breath.

"I've been granted a six-month post-doctoral fellowship at Haifa University." His voice held the same note of excitement I had heard in the past when he talked about his feelings for me.

"Oh." I worked at keeping my voice light, but couldn't hide my disappointment, never mind bring myself to congratulate him.

"I've always wanted to go to Israel, and I'll be studying with Haifa's expert on medieval Italian art. It's a great opportunity."

"I'm having second thoughts," I said, hurt and angry. "About us."

"Only six months, Claire. It'll go by fast."

"I'm happy for you if this is what you want." This was never going to work.

"I *do* want it, and I want you, too." Cake, and eat it.

"But it's how we met."

"A bit of fantastic luck," he said. Why wasn't he admitting to the personal ad? Our whole relationship was based on a lie, and he didn't have the courage to tell me the truth, that he had answered the ad, giving the impression that he was searching for a special someone and now he was leaving. For six months.

"By the way, I have some news, too. I went to the doctor's and you don't have to worry about any transmitted diseases."

"Oh. Good news."

Michael called several times, but I kept telling him I was too busy to get together. The part of me that waited by the phone for Max to call stopped. I thought maybe he would have a change of heart and recognize the error of his ways. How could he meet the love of his life and then abandon her? Me. But when December 13 arrived and I was officially forty-six, I felt a deep sadness overtake me. It was difficult to celebrate anything on the anniversary of my parents' death. I gathered my courage and called his cell. He answered on the first ring, but the connection was breaking up. He planned to visit his parents in Florida again before he set off for Haifa. Heavy static and the line went dead. When I tried his cell again, it was out of service, so I dialed his home number to leave a message. A woman answered and identified herself as Karen. "Max isn't here. Would you like to leave a message?"

My heart dropped like a stone down a deep well. "It's nothing. Nothing important." The way I remembered it, Max had made a clean break with Karen. So why in the world would she be answering his phone?

I imagined the phone conversation I would have had with my mother.

"Mom, I have a surprise for you."

"I love surprises."

"I'm pregnant."

Mom wouldn't miss a beat. "Are you happy about it, dear?"

"Most days, yes."

"One of those sperm banks?"

"No, Mom. Max is the father."

"Oh, my! This baby is going to be absolutely gorgeous!"

"This baby is going to be raised without a father unless things change. Max doesn't know about the baby, and I'm not sure how to tell him."

"May as well come right out with it."

"Mom, it's more complicated than that."

"Does it have to be?" she would have said with a sigh because one of her dreams had been to become a grandma.

It was a lazy morning. I ate ricotta cheese from the container and sat around in my pajamas watching romantic movies on TV. In the late afternoon, I dropped in on Josie.

Boccaccio was silent, concentrating on the view out the window.

"Back in his cage?"

"He'd rather observe the real live birds than those on TV, wouldn't you baby?"

"And maybe you're tired of watching him try to hang upside down?"

"There's that."

We spread peanut butter on pinecones and rolled them in seeds to pile in her window box. Then Josie opened a bag of hazelnuts and dumped them in a bowl with some dried figs. "From the Rialto this morning." On a platter, she carefully arranged Sicilian tangerines, their green leaves still clinging. "I'm going to miss this place, you know."

"And Boccaccio? How will he adjust?"

"Oh, I didn't tell you? He's coming with us! The *contessa* presented us with quite a generous going-away gift as a thank you for taking him off her hands. Besides, we've gotten pretty attached to him. Ethan bought a travel carrier and customized it with dowels for perches." She wrapped her arms around me and hugged me close to her. "Sure you'll be okay without me?"

"Of course I will."

"Everyone's going to be *so* happy," she said, patting me on the back.

Feeling less nauseous and more confident, I phoned Michael. "I'm finishing up a book due back at the publisher's," I said. I considered telling him that I was pregnant, that I had known the father-to-be for only a few days, and that these things happen. I could blame it on the mystical sunrise in the piazza, on the large, romantic moon the night of the flood. It was the magical atmosphere of Venice—the sky, water, and palaces—that were pulling me into a painting that may or may not include Max. It was possible that Max would become an under-drawing, part of the past instead of the picture. At this point, it was impossible to know how the painting that was my life would turn out. As much as I longed to confide in Michael, I didn't tell him any of this. Instead we talked about the excitement of the holidays, my writing, and his work.

I spent time reviewing the text and photographs of my copyedited manuscript. Vienna, Budapest, and Prague. Unlike Western Europeans who had lost their curiosity about Americans, those living in the old Iron Curtain countries were still receptive. I thumbed through the text for Vienna—the recipe for Mozart kugeln, a picture of the Riesenrad Ferris wheel used in the filming of *The Third Man*, a film shot in black and white, its plot full of gray areas, loaded with issues of trust, like whether someone would get pushed from the top of the wheel.

Next, a description of the Hundertwasser Museum with its uneven floors to remind the visitor that in life, while you need to watch your step, you must also trust your instinct and delight in the challenge.

Then Budapest—the hanging gardens, domes, and cupolas in the hills of Buda. And on the opposite bank, exotic Pest with its monuments and mineral baths. On the shores of the Danube, stalls of folk-designed pillows, aprons, and runners in reverse appliqué. Andrassy Avenue, with its cafés and bookstores, flowerbeds and fountains, and recipes for Gerbeaud's moist plum pie and cognac cherries in chocolate.

And finally, there was Prague—Mala Strana, the Charles Bridge, and the ancient Jewish cemetery. In the museum, crayoned butterflies drawn by children behind barbed wire at Terezin, victims of the ultimate betrayal.

On Christmas Day in Venice, the focus is on *la famiglia, l'amore e il cibo*—family, love, and food. Josie, Ethan, and I gathered at her place to enjoy wine and *crostini* with liver pâté followed by lamb roast with steamed vegetables.

Then we sat around the living room eating dessert—*panettone*, a light Milanese cake filled with candied fruit and raisins—and opening gifts.

In the stocking Josie handed me was a keychain with one of Man Ray's photographs, a can-can dancer, her cheeks sprinkled with glass tears. Deeper inside, a silk scarf designed by Escher, the mathematician who complained that his fellow colleagues became so fixated on how a gate opens that they failed to pass through it and venture into the gardens beyond. Escher's gardens were filled with birds that morphed into fish, floors that became ceilings, and stairways that tricked the imagination. His drawings played with the mind, and the mind played with the eyes, telling them what to see.

Next was a Chinese finger trap. My fingers went in easily enough, but the more I tried to pull free, the tighter they locked into place until I went against inclination, pushing my fingers toward each other and freeing them. When did she ever have the time to collect all this?

I received an email from Max that read:

> It's true that Jerusalem prays, Tel Aviv plays, and Haifa
> works. I've been spending most of my time researching early
> Italian art, but during short breaks I take a look around and
> realize what a beautiful place Mount Carmel is, with its lush
> green laurel, olive trees, the view of golden beaches and the blue

Mediterranean.

Yesterday I went with friends by Jeep to the National Park, and then on foot we followed a path to a cave where Neanderthal remains were found. There are several more caves where bands of robbers and the prophet Elijah hid out, and patches of forest that they refer to as "beauty spots." It's easy to see why they call this place the "vineyards of God." Please let me know how you are.

Max

I was left feeling vacant, disconnected. I replied that I had finished my book and was spending time with Josie and Ethan. Nothing else. After a quiet dinner together that evening, Josie, Ethan, and I strolled around the city. A rare sparkling snowfall transformed Venice into a setting from a Cornell dream, the one where a highwayman throws a panther skin on the cold, white ground and commands a ballerina to dance upon it. On a brick wall, someone had scrawled, *Cadeva dal cielo la neve . . . .* Down from heaven fell the snow with all its quietness. We reached Saint Mark's, its marble floor dusted as if with confectioner's sugar, softening any sound, and crossed the piazza, leaving a trail of footsteps.

20

Non c'é rosa senza spine.
There isn't a rose without a thorn.

A pop tune, *C'est trop triste Venise*, was playing on Nicole's radio. How sad Venice can be, when you've lost the love you discovered there. But I realized that I wasn't feeling sad. The night before, I'd dreamed that I was swimming the Grand Canal, like Byron, at night with the light of a full moon illuminating my path and all the windows of all the palaces twinkling like fireflies. My heart was full of love, and contentedness was a shore within sight.

"I'm auditing Professor Massini's class," Nicole said, opening her laptop to show me a streaming video of a Man Ray film. "He included this in one of his lectures."

On the monitor, a man and a woman walked down a path, arm in arm. They looked directly at me as if intending to continue right off the screen, cross the table, and perch themselves in the palm of my hand. They reminded me of my parents. The words "We are forever lost in the darkness of an eternal desert" flashed across the screen. The line of poetry summoned up the fears that Marco Polo harbored during his travels when he heard voices and didn't want to abandon his route for fear of dying. The words didn't fit with the image of the happy couple. Maybe it was all about juxtaposition.

Nicole poured me a cup of tea. "The professor mentioned a scandal in Paris, prints of Man Ray's work sold as originals. They used stolen negatives and blank paper from the thirties. And the tragedy is they can't prove a print isn't original without destroying the picture itself. *C'est dommage.*"

"Authenticity . . . " I was about to get on my high horse about Truth and Beauty, but couldn't ignore the nagging in my chest because I may have destroyed something beautiful with Max by taking it apart, all in the guise of getting to the truth.

The day after Christmas a package arrived from Michael, a V-neck sweater with wide horizontal stripes of antique rose, light blue, and pale pumpkin. He was thinking about me, a lot, his note read. We had a good chance of making it as a couple, and he hoped I felt the same. Michael was offering his love and was hopeful about a future together. I held the sweater up and checked myself out in the mirror, warmed not only by the soft yarns, but also by this wave of optimism and unconditional love.

Daniela called to apologize for such short notice, but she wanted to share her gift of two tickets for the Venice Simplon-Orient-Express. If possible, I was to join her in Paris where we could stay at the apartment she time-shared with the Massinis. Then we'd take the train back to Venice.

"Paris," I said in a call from the hotel, "I'd love to!" And I had always dreamed of riding on the luxury train. It took me less than an hour to reserve my Air France ticket and pack my bag. Daniela met me at De Gaulle, looking like a younger, invigorated version of herself. Zola, sporting a red sweater, danced a little dance.

We took a taxi to Saint-Germain-des-Prés and followed Zola's lead as she inspected each room in the apartment. In the pink galley at the end of the hallway, she wasted no time propping her front paws on the counter's edge and extending her sandpapery tongue to lap up some spilled sugar. Daniela scolded, but Zola couldn't resist one final stroke.

"Make yourself comfortable," Daniela said to me. "I'll brew us a pot of tea from the pantry."

The rooms, lacking the high ceilings and antique furnishings of a Venetian palazzo, were nevertheless rich, compact, and sleek. I nestled in a velvet loveseat by the window and arranged a cashmere throw over my legs. When Daniela carried in the tea tray, the room filled with the distinctive aroma of a campfire.

"Here's proof that some things *can* be hurried," she said. "When an occupying army prevented workers from slow drying the leaves, they sped up the process by arranging them over open fires. *E voilà*, lapsang souchong!" She pushed a pile of silk cushions aside and adjusted herself on the daybed opposite me.

"But I'm learning there are things that can't be rushed," I said, "like forming a loving relationship with a man."

"True, very true."

"Lately I feel like I've been thrashing around."

"Do you see that woman over there?" In the apartment window directly across from us, a young woman in tee shirt and tights moved in slow motion about the room. "Years ago, I studied Tai Chi," Daniela said, "like this woman. You see . . . she's practicing her cloud hands." The woman switched positions. "Now, bird flies into the forest." The woman thrust her hands forward. "Finally, she pushes the boat with the current. Each movement is a lesson in living. Gentle and yielding, the principle of life. Noodles and gunpowder weren't the only things Polo brought back from China."

Daniela filled my cup with smoky liquid. "We must operate from a place of calm because, otherwise, the truth can be scared away. If a person is peaceful, the truth will come to them."

In the morning, Daniela carried Zola in her arms until we got past the customers chugging down their espressos at the downstairs bar, while their lap dogs, tied to lampposts, sniffed each other.

"Window shopping for the French is *lèche-vitrines*," she said.

"So let's lick some windows!" We slowed to admire fairy-tale creations, Quimper ceramics, bolts of *toiles de Jouy*, and the fashionable clothes and accessories at Armani, Vuitton, and Hermès. We ended at the Luxembourg Gardens where we settled on a bench by the Fontaine Medici.

"They say there's a sadness in the air that you breathe here, in this exact spot," I said.

Daniela rubbed her hands together. "Really? I don't feel any of that. Only an impulse to warm myself."

"Would you think it strange if I told you that in Venice I'm sometimes followed by ghosts?"

"Oh well, Venice," Daniela said, with a wave of the hand. "Those poor souls become so attached to the city they simply can't bear to leave it."

"Then you're not shocked."

Zola, with her head propped on Daniela's foot, kept one eye on a pigeon that pecked at some crumbs.

"Not really. It seems to me they're most likely crying for attention. Like hungry children."

"They pop up in unexpected places, drop hints, and dish out advice."

"And perhaps it's good advice. After all, *i morti verze i oci ai vivi*. The dead open the eyes of the living. But if you ever want to be rid of them, you'd do well to leave them some treats."

"Like cookies for Santa?"

"Something like that, yes. Food for the souls of the dead."

"Like Egyptians, with bread and beer," I said.

"Celts with mead and meat."

"Buddhists' rice and sesame seeds."

"And let's not forget the Romans—cake and wine," Daniela added, laughing.

"The best for last."

"And with that in mind," she said, rising from the bench, "I'm going to buy you the best apple strudel in the world, to feed your spirit."

"Strudel in Paris?"

"You'll see. Oh, these French and their magnificent dishes!"

In the old Jewish section called the Marais, at 7 Rue des Rosiers, we found Jo Goldenberg's Deli and were greeted at the door by a fantail pigeon cooing in its wicker cage. From behind the counter, Jo gave Daniela a big smile and, after introductions, he waggled a finger at me. "Be prepared. People who come in here weep."

"He means weep for joy once they've tasted his chopped liver and chicken soup," Daniela explained, "but most of all, his strudels."

While Jo selected delicacies for us, I was drawn to a wall of faded, creased black and white photographs, all in their dark frames: a woman in well-cut dress and feathered hat, a bearded man in dress trousers and suspenders, girls with bows in their hair, somber expressions on their young faces.

"The family he lost at Auschwitz," Daniela whispered. "His mother, father, all his sisters."

Jo was watching a chef-in-training as the young man rolled out pastry and stretched it over the back of his hand. "Thin enough to read a love letter through," Jo reminded the young man. We continued to observe as, in slow and deliberate steps, the intern laid the pastry out on a tea towel, spooned filling in the sheet of dough, rolled it and put it in the oven.

Jo presented me with a fresh-baked strudel on waxed paper, and as I took my first bite, my eyes teared up. "See? You can't say I didn't warn you!" He took Daniela's elbow and led us to a table where, stooping, he placed a small bowl of beef goulash in front of Zola. "Not too spicy," he said, in a reassuring voice.

Daniela, savoring her strudel, surveyed the room. "When the Israelis kicked Arafat out of Lebanon, terrorists tossed a grenade in here and gunned down thirty people. That particular day . . . " She stopped and pressed her hand to her forehead.

"Daniela?" I reached out to her.

"Even after all these years." Her eyes filled. "My friend, my lover, Alberto. He was picking up an order for us here at Jo's. I stayed in the apartment, watching television, when they broke in to announce the attack. It was . . . " Her voice broke. "My Alberto had been killed."

Goosebumps rose along my arms, and my whole body offered up an involuntary shiver. I put my arm around my friend's shoulder, my face close to hers. "I am so, so sorry," I whispered.

"I found—and lost—the love of my life." Zola lapped her mistress's hand. "I came here once on the anniversary of the assassinations, brought flowers and filled my ears with that sad Jewish music. But it's better to visit Jo's this way, with you. *L'chaim*, to life." When she lifted her cup of tea, I tapped it with my own.

After bidding Jo goodbye, we continued in the direction of the Place des Vosges and Daniela told me more about Alberto. "His father was Roman, garrulous; his mother Danish, blonde and refined. On his apartment walls hung a collection of Royal Copenhagen plates with the dearest pictures—a cat on a windowsill, children awaiting the Christmas train, geese hunting for grain in the snow, all blueprints for longing. In those days, Paris was so different," she said. "Families living outside with only scraps of furniture, couples making love under the bridges. These days the buildings are scrubbed clean, the sidewalks washed every day."

We reached the square, once used for jousting tournaments. Now it was empty, except for four sections of boxwood arranged like the mounting corners in a scrapbook, as if one picture had been torn from them and they awaited another. It turned out that loss was no stranger to Daniela, either. The nagging heartache of having lost a loved one continued to linger with her, too; yet she carried on, made beautiful books that people loved, and put a bright face on every day.

That night, a mix of static and pop music drifted from the radio in Daniela's room. Some French, some English, and then Gino Paoli singing about *un gusto amaro di cose perdute*, the bitter taste of things lost. I never did feel bitter about losing my parents. I felt devastated, crushed, robbed—so there was anger, yes, but bitterness, no. They had been the best of parents, and I held on to the happy memories of shared moments. I hadn't listened to the recording of their voices since that fateful day at the cemetery, but that was okay because I carried my parents with me. And Bernie? Yes, that day at the cemetery did leave a bad taste in my mouth. And yes, I'll admit it, concerning Bernie, I did feel some bitterness still . . .

We slept in, taking our first meal at Les Deux Magots, the literary café named for the wooden statues of Chinese mandarins that dominate the room. The haunting fragrance of coffee perfumed the air. Two dark-skinned men dressed like princes in long flowing white robes were exiting after having deposited a single peanut at each table.

"Picasso, Hemingway, de Beauvoir, and Sartre were regulars," Daniela was saying, as we took in the view of busy Boulevard Saint Germain from our table. She shelled the peanut and offered it to me.

"Sartre said life was looking out a car window, with everything coming into focus somewhere down the road," I said as the veiled mist of a Gauloise circled my glass of citron pressé, then drifted in the direction of Daniela's black coffee.

"That's why one must take advantage of every scenic pull-off."

"Did he say that?"

"No, but he should have." She finished her coffee and cast her gaze around the room as the two princely men, confident that their samples had proved irresistible, re-entered the café carrying large baskets with bags of peanuts for sale. "The upper crust has fled across the street to the Flore. Now it's all publishers and people watchers at Les Deux Magots."

"Let's not forget pregnant travel writers."

"How could we possibly?"

We lingered along the riverbank to browse the bookstalls stocked with their postcards, maps, and old prints before continuing on to the Samaritaine, the city's largest department store.

Inside La Samar we spent our time in cosmetics, choosing Roger & Gallet soaps—exotic Vetiver, hinting of India in June, and extra vieille with its lingering rosemary. Caravaggio could keep his knife—I would sleep with a fragrant soap under my pillow. We climbed to the rooftop terrace to take in the panoramic view of Paris—the Conciergerie where Marie Antoinette was kept before her beheading, our neighborhood marked by the spire of the Saint-Germain-des-Prés church, the Notre Dame with its flying buttresses, the Eiffel Tower, and the white marble Sacre Coeur.

"I'd like to visit Alberto's grave at the Père Lachaise," Daniela said. "Would you mind?"

The cemetery meant betrayal and heartache to me, but as I watched a *bateau mouche* cruise the Seine, slipping beneath the Pont Neuf, I replied, "No, not at all."

It was standing room only when we boarded the Métro. Zola nestled in her tote as Daniela and I held onto leather straps.

"The last time I rode the Métro," Daniela said, "I had an unpleasant experience, a tug at my shoulder, and when I looked down, fingers groping inside my bag. I delivered a hard chop to the wrist and Zola launched into her attack mode."

"Was he apprehended?"

She shook her head. "He looked like any commuting businessman and quickly joined an accomplice coming from the other direction. They managed to exit just as the doors closed. Poor Zola peed a puddle of exasperation."

"That's awful." I bristled at the thought of pickpockets and their slimy tactics, and had devoted a whole chapter to them in my book. In Barcelona they squirt fake pigeon droppings on you and do a whole, oh-let-me-help-you routine while they reach for your bag. In Russia, thugs hide a razor blade against the roof of the mouth and use it to slit open your purse.

Daniela bought flowers at the cemetery's entrance, and we took a leisurely walk, commenting on the monuments along our path. But as we approached Oscar Wilde's grave, I got caught up in disturbing memories of Bernie and Eric and had to fight the tide of anger that built inside me. When Daniela remarked on the notes left by admirers, my eyes swept over the tombstone, resting on a glint that winked in the sunlight by the carved foot. Someone had recovered the memory card from my smashed cell phone and placed it there. I picked up the slender wafer and held it tight, then slipped it into my pocket. My heart filled with the relief of recovering a lost treasure, and by the time we reached the tomb of Victor Noir, I was exuberant. From her bunch of flowers, Daniela offered me a narcissus to place in Victor's hat as a sign of thanks.

We continued on to Héloïse and Abélard, the tomb most resonant of romance linked with tragedy, skipped that ominous day in October. Dark images raced through my mind. He: unhappy with Héloïse's pregnancy. She: not wanting a forced marriage. He: retreating to a monastery. She: entering a convent. "I never read a letter from you," her quill scratched across paper, "without the immediate feeling we are together. *Vale, unice.* Farewell, my one and only."

Alberto's grave was marked with the carved figure of a man holding an open book. Daniela brushed some debris from the stone and placed her flowers at the statue's feet. Zola paced back and forth, whining to move on, but the two of us stood quietly, heads bowed. Daniela murmured, "*Arrivederci, tesoro.*" It was time to say goodbye, to let go. I turned the memory card over and over in my pocket, then kneeling beside the stone, I took it out and held it in my palm. "Daniela, would you mind?"

"Not at all," she answered.

Pressing the card against the stone, I pushed it deep into the soil, and put my parents to rest.

When we reached the Holocaust memorials, Daniela chose a white pebble from the path and placed it on the base of the monument in remembrance of Buchenwald victims.

"A token monument," she said, "to show that someone came and remembered. Love and memory, strong and enduring as a rock."

I remembered an afternoon when Max and I lounged in bed talking about artists, filmmakers, poets and writers, and their power to change the world. "Oliver Wendell Holmes was an anti-Semite," Max told me. "But then one night at the theater, he sat hemmed in by Jews, the very people he was taught to think of as 'hook-nosed kites in carrion clothes.' And sitting there, he couldn't ignore their dark hair and gentle eyes, and it occurred to him that Jesus must have resembled these people. When that happened, he said a shadow floated from his soul." Max had turned to me then, holding my reflection in his deep brown eyes. "'From thee the son of Mary came, with thee the Father deigned to dwell. Peace be upon thee, Israel'—his words."

I pressed my hand on my tummy and stooped to pick up a stone.

We were about to exit the cemetery when I said, "Daniela, one more thing. I'd like to go to Eric's shop. Bernie works there, and I have something to say to him, face to face."

"*Va bene,*" she said, hailing a taxi. "I'll have you dropped off, circle the Arc de Triomphe, and return for you."

Bernie was in the window, jamming a baguette in the crotch of a mannequin's skintight leather pants, and when I rapped my knuckles on the glass, he looked up and froze, his face free of expression, like a mannequin himself. I swung the door open with enough force to set off a clatter of tinkling bells, then marched up to the curved platform while Eric stared from behind the register, trying to keep up glib chitchat with two young men buying leather jackets.

"Let's step outside, Claire." It was Bernie's whispering that triggered my rage and caused me to snap.

"You son of a bitch!" I yelled.

Bernie made a run for the door, upending the mannequin. I chased him out onto the sidewalk, swinging my bag at him.

"How could you do that to me?" I yelled. "How could you lie and cheat and then expect me to feel sorry for you? You're so self-involved, you never did apologize!" I could feel my vocal chords shredding. When a dozen pedestrians stopped to watch the show, Bernie pulled his jacket over his head for protection, or anonymity.

"I wasn't sure until I met Eric," he pleaded from under cover. This was my cue to go after him again, so I took a couple more roundhouse swings with my bag.

"I'm sorry, Claire. I'm truly, truly sorry!" Bernie peeked out from under the jacket. "Please, forgive me."

Eric came running out. "I've phoned the police!"

Just then, the taxi careened up to the curb. When Daniela threw the passenger door open, Zola dashed from her hold, raced toward us, and bit Bernie in the ankle. Then she ran back and jumped into Daniela's arms. I climbed into the cab, and we drove away, sirens wailing in the distance.

"Well, that's that," Daniela said, offering Zola a doggie treat. "Out with the old."

At the Gare de L'Est, chefs in tall white hats gathered on the platform collecting lobsters for the trip. When the shrill whistle of the stationmaster pierced the air, Zola trembled. A white-gloved steward took a picture of us standing on the red carpet at the steps of the Venice Simplon-Orient-Express, and then helped us aboard. "Your carriage once served as staff car for Winston Churchill," he said, leading us to our cabin.

Daniela admired the brass fittings of our compartment, "You'll like this, Claire. All the slots of the screws line up vertically. Now, that's craftsmanship. And the history! Imagine the messengers with their briefcases chained to their wrists, the thieves and spies, and the king of Bulgaria taking over the engine and racing the train into Sofia."

Soon the train left the station and, as it picked up speed, we rocked to the thu-thunk, thu-thunk of its rhythm. "We'll bring back some caviar just for you," Daniela told Zola, leaving her with a bowl of water.

It was New Year's Eve, *il capodanno*, and following our sumptuous dinner in l'Etoile du Nord, champagne corks popped all around us.

Back in our cabin, Daniela climbed into the top bunk of the converted compartment seats, and Zola, afraid of heights, scampered into the bottom bunk with me, snuggling at my feet. I wondered where Max and Michael were and how they were greeting the New Year. Halfway through the night, I reached down and pulled Zola into my arms. Practicing for baby, I sang a lullaby in her furry ear.

In the morning, we passed the sunlit slopes of the Alps, and my breath caught as we arrived in Venice on the first day of the New Year. In with the new.

From the railway station, we caught the *Numero Uno* to the Gritti Palace where I curled up with a book while Daniela made a few phone calls.

"The Massinis have invited us for cocktails this evening. In the meantime, would you like to take a leisurely walk to the Florian for a little treat?"

On our way out, we stopped by the kitchen to say hello to Chef Nicolò. He was exuberant in his wishes for a Happy New Year and kissed our faces, over and over. When we reached the Florian and gazed from the tearoom at the sun-splashed square, the cloudless sky, Daniela said, "This is what heaven must be like."

"I thought by the expression on your face that you were in heaven when Chef was kissing you."

Daniela blushed, stirred the sugar in her tea, and changed the subject, summarizing the front-page story from the *Gazz* delivered to us by the waiter. "'Two Neapolitans Snagged in Art Theft Net. An inspector set up a sting operation, and caught *due piccioni con una fava*, two pigeons with one bean, after receiving a tip from a tourist'—that's you, I believe—'about a suspicious man who leased a local antique shop.' These pigeons, by the way, look very familiar." She held up the page featuring mug shots of Gianni and the hawker of amateur art from outside the Guggenheim. "What a pair! Remember, *La luce! La luce!* They were placed under surveillance following your complaint. 'An undercover police officer assigned to visit the shop made a request for an ancient Attic artifact, specifically, a satyr holding a wine cup. It is alleged that this shopkeeper acted as the fence for stolen artifacts. From his place of business, the police recovered Etruscan antiquities, Venetian paintings, Roman sculpture . . .'" She put the paper down and tore into her croissant.

"Busy boys," I said.

"They keep the black market flourishing." Her lips glistening, she returned to the article. "'Over the past thirty years, the police have recovered more than half a million artifacts and works of art.'"

"According to Max, stolen art is most often found close to home."

"True. Frescoes from a floor in Pompeii—one, a Cupid and, the other, a rooster pecking a pomegranate—were recovered less than half a mile from the site. But other times, the police are forced to search for leads in the shadowy world of the *tombaroli*."

"Grave robbers?"

She nodded. "And from there, they go to unscrupulous dealers and any auction house or private collector who's willing to turn a blind eye. At the top of the ladder is the museum. But it begins with the *tombaroli*. This piece, for example. The police describe it as incredible and precious."

"Well, let's hope they keep both pigeons in the cage for a long, long time. You know, Daniela, I met this thief up close and personal."

"That day he brushed by us."

I shook my head.

"What do you mean, then?"

"He showed me around Torcello and came to my room that night with the stolen goods. He managed to turn off the lights, drop his pants and try to attack me." Zola cocked her head and rotated her ears.

"Not as harmless as he looks, this one." Daniela gave the newspaper's picture of Gianni a hard snap with her fingers.

The gate that Max opened weeks ago had been left ajar in anticipation of our arrival at the Massinis. Isabella greeted us at the door and led us up marble stairs to the *piano nobile* where a mirror caught the last bit of light flickering through the windows. As she took my coat, she made a point of telling me that Max spoke of me fondly. "Have you heard from him recently?" she wanted to know.

"He keeps in touch."

She introduced her brother-in-law, Carlo, a classically handsome young man with clear olive skin, his ponytail and eyes the color of honey. He joined Daniela and me as we admired a view of the Canal that rivaled a Canaletto painting.

"To wake up each morning to this," I said.

"Oh, you get used to it. Like anything else." He sounded world-weary, a Euro-sophisticate.

"Carlo studies architecture," Daniela said.

"At the University of Venice," he added.

"And what do you do for fun?"

"I take photographs. Many photographs. May I show you?" He led the two of us to a brocaded silk sofa, and from beneath a coffee table that held a dozen *millefiori* paperweights—among them, I noted, the heart from the Guggenheim museum shop—he pulled a leather-bound album. "Family and friends," he said, resting it on my lap and pausing at portraits of himself with a bearded friend, fleeting images printed on rice paper. "We, *come si dice*"—the corners of his mouth turned down—"we don't see each other anymore."

"Ah," Daniela said.

"And here," he said, turning the page, "little moments." Zola, her tongue flicking at Daniela's face. An aproned Isabella preparing a dish in the kitchen. "And here . . . " he continued. My eyes locked on a man at a table outside the Florian. Cleft chin, dark eyes. "Max." Carlo followed my gaze.

"Max," Daniela said, taking a closer look. Carlo continued to turn the pages, but I barely noticed the rest of the photos in the album.

"Claire," Carlo said. "Would you allow me to photograph you?"

"I'd be honored."

"I'm going to look for *il professore*," Daniela said.

While Carlo disappeared to get his camera, I adjusted my clothes and then on a whim, undid my braid and brushed my hair loose. And when the camera began to click, Carlo, trying for a certain expression, said, "Think of something just beyond your reach." That was easy.

When we were finished, I took a small bottle of Pellegrino from Isabella's tray and wandered into the study just off the reception room. The professor had a corner office with a view of the Grand Canal from the front window and, from the side, a narrow canal and adjacent palazzo. Daniela was examining a blanket-sized map that covered most of the wall. A red pushpin marked the location of the Parisian apartment at Saint-Germain-des-Prés.

"No professor?" I asked.

"He'll be right out. He's watching the last scene in *Jules and Jim*. Fascinating film."

"Carlo's sweet."

"And able to coax his subjects into revealing themselves," Daniela said. "By the way, you look *favolosa* with your hair like that. Wild and beautiful."

Irma, a petite guest in her fifties, entered the room and handed a tea-colored manuscript to Daniela. "From San Lazzaro," she said. And for my benefit, "Where Byron studied Armenian with the monks."

Maybe. Insiders know that although the Saint Lazarus monks invite tourists to visit the room that Byron occupied, they never show specimens of the Armenian exercises he wrote. Some suggest he secluded himself in the monastery because gin was unattainable, making it the perfect place to dry out, and that Byron only pretended to learn Armenian. Still, San Lazzaro was an island of interest with its welcoming statue of Saint Lazarus, the patron saint of lepers, and its screeching peacocks.

The Massinis entered the room, and the conversation turned to *Jules and Jim*.

"We all want an exciting partner but, at the same time, one who is stable and committed," the professor was saying. "A combination nearly impossible to find in the same person."

"Truffaut does a fine job examining the contradictions that exist in love affairs," Isabella said.

"Moreau's character wants a pure relationship, free of hypocrisy and compromise," said Professor Massini.

"But don't you think she goes too far when she drives Jim and herself off the broken arch of a bridge?" Isabella said.

Everyone seemed to be pondering that question when Irma mentioned that her aunt left her home to move in with a daughter, and that the family was searching for someone to apartment-sit. They all turned to me.

"Would this place interest you?" Daniela asked.

When I answered that I'd love to take a look at it, knowing glances were exchanged.

The aunt's apartment was located in the Castello district—the tail of the fish—off the pedestrian mall called Via Garibaldi, a former canal that Napoleon filled in with rocks.

"Only Italian is spoken here," Daniela said as we passed an old man and his cat asleep on a bench. "No tourists."

We climbed the stairs to the second floor and examined the spacious rooms. The drapes and sofa were outlined with light that spilled from the windows and splashed onto the marble floors. The stark walls were blank pages. I saw myself drinking coffee at the table, cooking pasta on the small gas stove, writing at the desk. I saw myself gazing from the French windows with a baby in my arms, watching children play tag on a bridge with no worry of knocking a tourist into the water. I saw my future. It felt so right to begin the next chapter of my life here, in this apartment. *The Seven Year Itch* might continue to play at Dolce e Gabbana, but my life was not going to be a fuzzy film stuck in an uninterrupted loop.

"Daniela, let me treat you to dinner."

"*Molto bene*, but first, I must stop by the Gritti to get something."

When we arrived at her room, Daniela went to the armoire and emerged with a chocolate-trimmed orange box, saying, "For you and your baby."

"Daniela . . . " Inside was a deep red Birkin bag. "I'm overwhelmed." The scent of fine leather filled the air.

"Given to me years ago, but it never really suited." She brushed the tissue paper aside. "Look, enough room for diapers and bottles."

"It's incredible." I had to sit down. When Daniela placed the Birkin in my lap, I traced the gold hardware with my finger. "But I don't deserve it."

"Fortunately, I'll be the judge of that." She held her palms out. "Remember, stay open to things that come your way." She unzipped an inner pocket. "And look here, a new cell phone. You shouldn't be running around the city without this, especially in your condition."

We freshened up and enjoyed a lavish meal in the hotel dining room. When we placed our order for tea, Chef Nicolò made an appearance at our table, presenting us with plates of black and white chocolate soufflé. "Fresh from the oven and lighter than air," he said. "May I?" He pulled up a seat and joined us, a bottle in his hand. "Moscato d'Asti, a lovely dessert wine from Piemonte." He poured three glasses. "Fragrant and mildly sweet." Keeping his eyes on Daniela, he offered a toast, "To two beautiful ladies. *Cin cin.*" I took a tiny sip, enough to wet my lips, while the chef finished his wine with dispatch, and hustled back to his kitchen.

Tucked beside each soufflé we discovered a tiny, red candy heart and inside each dessert, little pockets of melted semi-sweet chocolate.

"Think a romantic heart beats beneath that bib apron?" I said.

Daniela answered only with a smile.

My New Year's resolution was to stay put and take care of myself, to experience *dolce far niente*, the sweetness of doing nothing. I let the phrase roll around on my tongue like Asti Spumante. I wrote to Max about my decision to remain in Venice, but he did not reply. Fine, I thought.

At the apartment, guests came and went: Nicole with a basket of herbs, Carlo with a framed print of my picture, Daniela with a decorated hand mirror, Michael with a perfect pineapple from the Via Garibaldi market. "To set by your door now that you're home." Like Proust, my dream had become, quite simply, my address.

Irma stopped by to see how I was doing and to invite me the following morning to her celebration of the Epiphany. Her place overlooked the Rialto Bridge and the Grand Canal, she said, and offered a splendid view that included the annual regatta. My apartment filled with the warm vibrations of gifts, shared meals, conversations, and now, invitations.

Morning came, bright and clear. At Irma's place, several guests hovered around a table of assorted pastries and fruits, while others stood by the windows, cups of coffee in hand. I found Carlo out on the balcony preparing to photograph the senior members of the oldest Venetian boating society.

"They're all in drag," I said, as rowers, dressed in long skirts, shawls, and kerchiefs, raced special skiffs and gondolas up the Grand Canal.

"Dressed as *La Befana*. Legend says it was at her house that the Magi stopped to ask directions. When they invited her to join in their search for a newborn king, she was sweeping her floor and said she had too many chores."

"And these men use brooms in place of oars?"

"You are meant to believe," Carlo said, offering me his camera. "But look through the lens, and you'll see that in fact their oars are wrapped in twigs to resemble broomsticks."

I made out the patterned fabrics, the craggy faces, the disguised oars used by the rowers, some single and others in teams of two or more. They had set off from the Palazzo Balbi in San Tomà and were making their way toward the Rialto Bridge where a gigantic sock was hung. "So what happened to this witchy old woman?"

"She changed her mind and tried to follow, but lost her way. Now she wanders the planet forever in search of baby Jesus, and when she comes across any sleeping child, she leaves a gift, just in case it is *il Neonato*, the newborn king."

"Riding a broom?"

Carlo nodded. "And sliding down the chimney with her bag of presents to stuff stockings for the *bambini*. So we see *La Befana* as quite charming."

"You'll get some great pictures from this spot."

"I'm hoping they run one or two in the *Gazz*."

I began to see more of Michael. He was working in Mestre for a few weeks and was free on Wednesdays. That day became the high mark of my week, like the midpoint on a bridge, a vantage point from which I could learn more about the city and its "beauty spots." Inspired by Carlo, I wanted to take lots of pictures, so we packed food and film, and began each Wednesday together at Piazza San Marco.

"Did you notice we're the only ones with cameras? Venetians will carry umbrellas, newspapers, briefcases, but this?" Michael said, holding up his Nikon. "Never."

"Then we'll be recognized as visitors. But that's okay."

We photographed purposeful women in their sensible shoes, men gathered to smoke cigars and share stories, shoppers pulling carts of groceries. We snapped students lugging books and friends who walked with their arms around each other, talking politics and theater. Sometimes we met Nicole for lunch, and she and Michael fell into easy conversation about fashion, music, raising a family. My week fell into its own comfortable rhythm of taking pictures, shopping from vendors at the Rialto and along the Fondamenta della Sensa, and cooking at my small gas stove. I experimented with every kind of risotto. *Risi e bisi, risi e funghi, risi e sepe.* I learned to prepare fat pink scampi, lilac-striped sole, and silvery sardines—dishes so beautiful that I took pictures of them. Michael would often come to dinner, carrying a bottle of wine or a bouquet of flowers, and after we ate, we did the dishes together and then talked late into the evening.

As I walked around the city, I let my eyes wander upward to a world of rooftop gardens, frescoes, friezes, and family crests that I'd never before noticed. That is how one morning I discovered Saint Martin carved in high relief above the door of a priest's home close to the San Martino Church. The soldier was stained by time, his sword and foot broken off and lost. But he was on horseback and didn't need his foot. And someone had cared enough to patch the white marble with resins to prevent further cracking. It was true: Every day something was lost in Venice. There was always something to be retrieved, cleaned, mended, and cherished. Once upon a time I wanted everything to be perfect and in order, but life isn't like that. Life is like Venice.

Apple Strudel

2 1/2 cups all-purpose flour
1/4 teaspoon salt
2 egg yolks
3 tablespoons vegetable oil
6 ounces warm water

Filling:
8 apples, chopped
1/2 cup lemon juice
1 cup granulated sugar
2 tablespoons cinnamon
1 cup golden raisins
1 cup toasted bread crumbs
8 tablespoons butter, melted

Sift flour and salt in a mixing bowl. Create a well in the center of the flour. In a separate bowl, whisk the eggs, 2 tablespoons oil, and water.

Pour the liquid into the well of flour, and turning the bowl, work in with a fork.

Once the dough comes together, knead it.

Continue kneading for 15 minutes until satiny.

Coat the outside with 1 tablespoon vegetable oil and cover in plastic wrap.

Let stand for 20 minutes (enough time to write a love letter).

Remove plastic wrap.

Preheat the oven to 375 degrees F.

In a small bowl, combine the sugar and cinnamon.

In a medium bowl, toss the apples with lemon juice. Add the cinnamon sugar along with the raisins to the apples. Set aside.

Place the dough on a floured tea towel. With a rolling pin, roll the dough to a 12-inch square.

Lift the dough from the table and work it with the back of the hand, constantly moving the hands, pulling the dough until it stretches very thin. Thin enough to read a love letter placed beneath it. Place on a sheet pan.

Spray the dough with melted butter.

Place 1/2 cup breadcrumbs on the stretched dough, 3 inches wide and 3 inches from the edge.

Place the prepared apples on top of the crumbs, then sprinkle with the remaining 1/2 cup crumbs.

Roll up carefully. With a knife, trim the ends of the dough and tuck them under.

Spray with melted butter.

Bake for 20 minutes.

Spray with butter, and turn the sheet pan around.

Continue to bake for another 20 minutes until golden brown.

Have a hankie ready in case of tears.

21

Lontan dagli occhi, lontan dal cuore.
Far from the eyes, far from the heart.

My second trimester was comfortable, no nausea, just a swelling abdomen. And then it happened. I felt a terrible cramp that nearly knocked me to the floor. I rushed to the doctor, but by then the pain had lifted. He ordered an ultrasound and checked for an assortment of possible ailments. Everything looked fine, but he advised me to take it easy, to avoid quick changes in position, and to bend toward the pain to relieve it. He recommended warm baths, getting enough fluids, and walking. Walking was good.

I couldn't imagine losing this child. I thought back to the important people in my life who were gone. My parents, Bernie—well, good riddance to him—and now I wondered whether I'd ever see Max again.

One morning as Michael and I drank hot chocolate at the Florian, I told him about the pregnancy.

He set his cup in its saucer, and became very quiet. Finally, he managed to say, "Claire, I have to tell you, I'm crushed, because I thought . . . "

"I know, Michael. I'm sorry."

His eyes misted, and his gaze wandered to the corner of the room. When I put my hand on his, he cleared his throat and turned to face me, his eyes clear. He surprised me by saying, "But, you know what? It doesn't matter whose baby it is. I'm here for you, Claire. I always will be." He leaned over and gave me a kiss on the cheek, and I thought that maybe he was the best kind of risk taker, taking a chance on me.

From then on, he reached for my hand whenever we took the stairs up and down bridges. He rested his open palm on my back when we entered buildings as if to shepherd me in, pulled out my chair for me, and gazed at me in an adoring way.

It became our routine to stop by the Libreria Acqua Alta in Castello where books written in every language were stowed in gondolas, rowboats, and a gleaming porcelain tub, all moored on the wide floorboards of a large, open room. One afternoon we browsed through the picture books where a sleepy tuxedo cat roused himself, listening to Michael as he read one of the stories aloud. Two small children gravitated toward him, drawn in by the tale. At the open back door came the sound of the water from the canal gently licking the stone step. A sense of contentment swept over me. This was a world that I wished for my baby-to-be. Beauty, peace, and a kind and loving presence.

I think it was a moment similar to Cornell's at the Automat, but the springboard for me wasn't a piece of pie behind a glass door; it was Michael's voice transporting me to a land of picture books, comfy chairs, sleepy cats, and small children. From that day on, I began to compose a different kind of photograph, one that reflected the way my world had shifted. The Little Market of Miracles was spilling with paper goods that would add another dimension to my photo collages. Delicate napkins from tearooms, opera tickets from La Fenice, biscotti wrappers from bakeries. *Cianfrusaglie,* Daniela called them, found items of value to no one else, but precious to the artist. She advised me on the use of letterpress, embossing, engraving, and die cutting, and soon an alphabet book called *Sounds of Venice* began to take shape.

One morning, after purchasing some old postcards, ancient advertisements, and a beautiful soap wrapper at the market, I visited the Santa Maria dei Miracoli and thanked the Madonna for answering my prayers and helping me to forgive Josie and Max, and for bringing Michael into my life.

Feeling serene, I left the church and cast an eye at *Sior Rioba*. A little note taped to the edge of his sleeve fluttered and threatened to blow away. I made a move to attach it more securely, but on second thought, I opened it. A young woman is torn because she feels that her beloved is *brutto*, ugly. Overcome by a Dear Abby impulse, I scribbled a response. "*Amore è cieco . . .*" Love is blind, but sees afar. And so began a new pastime of mine, dishing out brain candy. I didn't worry one bit about the Italian admonition not to "give counsel or salt till asked." All these little notes represented cries for help, and with that in mind, I stored extra Baci sayings in my coat pocket so that if a proverb didn't immediately come to mind, I could answer with one of those sweet little slips of paper.

I went home and worked on my first picture book. The handwritten lyrics came from a traditional song that my mother used to sing to me when I was small.

I kissed the rose and the rose kissed me,
fragrant as only a rose can be.
Please take the kiss that comforts me
back to the one I love.

I made a night sky the deep blue of an Evening in Paris bottle, a moon as full as the one Max and I saw from the bridge during *acqua alta*, a red rose like the one we kissed the morning we met. Satisfied that I could market such books, I continued to troll the flea markets and antique shops for scraps that would inspire.

When Michael wasn't in Venice, he called every day and sent frequent gifts of baby sweaters, booties, and knitted caps. Max wrote to tell me about his participation in an event organized by the Dante Alighieri Society in Jerusalem. His research was going well, and he also found time to go to the Haifa Cinémathèque to see international films.

Daniela called from Milan. "I spend most of the day cutting and pasting," I told her. "When something doesn't work, I remind myself . . . endless possibilities. Life's just one big bowl of Baci."

"And our bowls overfloweth." Daniela sounded happier than ever.

While Pierre spent his days at the National Library and Etienne at school, Nicole devoted her time to her baby, Françoise, who had arrived at the end of January. We took turns pushing the carriage around the city.

One morning we met Pierre in the library reading room to view the *mappamundi*, the fifteenth-century circular map of the world. An enormous bust of Petrarch presided over balconies of books that reached all the way to the ceiling.

"Fra Mauro died while making a copy for Venice, so Bianco completed this one, discovered in the monastery of Murano," the attendant told us as he led us behind a curtain in the back gallery.

"Mauro didn't travel," Pierre said, as we studied the parchment map. "He drew the world as others described it, sometimes the way they remembered it from a passing ship. And he used Polo's notes, as well. Fra Mauro spent his life trying to create an accurate map of the world, but he had to be satisfied with guesswork and sketchy impressions."

"He must have been very trusting," I said, pointing to the six-foot map. "Look at this, he's put the South on top!" Topsy-turvy, so much for relying on others who can turn your world upside down.

As we left the library, a woman stopped to admire Françoise. "What a sweet little mouth, perfect as the O in Giotto," she said.

Nicole and I knew the story, how the Pope's courier came to Giotto's studio in search of the best painter. In response, Giotto laid down a sheet of paper, dipped his brush in red paint and, with a flick of his wrist, made a perfect circle. The pope gave Giotto the commission.

"That story is a good reminder that things don't always have to be complicated to be perfect," Nicole said, casting me a sideways glance.

On an afternoon after shooting pictures, Michael and I were returning home on the *Numero Uno* when the wind picked up and tore away a corner of the *trompe l'oeil* canvas that covered the Ca' Foscari's façade during its restoration. The gusts grew increasingly violent until our waterbus twisted out of control and traveled sideways down the Grand Canal.

"My God, Michael! What's going on?" I yelled, trying to steady myself and to keep my scarf from blowing away. The *vaporetto* continued off its course, smashing into a pair of gondolas moored to poles and splintering them.

"The *bora*," he shouted as he struggled to maintain his balance and to help me keep mine. "From the Russian steppes. I heard it's especially violent this winter."

We disembarked at San Marco and ducked into a small restaurant, hoping to warm up. Once we joined some locals sitting at the bar, we were cheered by the aromas drifting from the kitchen and ordered the traditional sardines cooked with raisins and vinegar, served with grilled white polenta. While we waited in anticipation for our meals, we heard singing and noticed Angelo, celebrating with his family. He called hello to us and continued to serenade us all with sea songs from the eighteenth century. When we applauded, he ordered a round of grappa for everyone.

"What do you hear from Max these days?" Michael said, downing his drink.

"He's continuing his research, going to movies and such, and maintains his usual carefree attitude about everything. It bothers me that he hasn't been straightforward about the way he and I met, that he hasn't said anything about that personal ad run by Josie. How can I trust him? I'm not telling him about the pregnancy, not now anyway." Michael frowned. "Of course, I will when the time comes. But I really don't like being misled. Josie's apologized. But Max hasn't admitted to anything. I'm wary of false beginnings," I said, sounding like Ruskin. The whole time I was talking, Michael fidgeted. I was sorry to make him uncomfortable with my complaints, felt a rush of affection for him, and gave him a reassuring smile. "I like things to happen naturally. Like the two of us," I said, taking his hand and gently squeezing it.

But he pulled away, folding his hands on the table in the way I imagined he must do at his business meetings when things are not going smoothly. "There's something that's been eating away at me, Claire, and now I realize how unfair I've been to Max, and to you."

"Unfair to Max?"

"Josie swore me to secrecy, and I didn't want to create more conflict in your friendship."

"Josie?"

"I hope you won't be too angry with me, Claire. I thought we were a perfect match, and once I met you, I was sure of it."

"A perfect match?" I was beginning to sound like Boccaccio on a bad day, but I had no idea what Michael was talking about. I only knew that it was making me uneasy.

"That's what I'm trying to tell you, Claire. *I* was the one who was supposed to meet you at Saint Mark's."

"*What?*"

"The Benetton people threw a party the night before, and when one of the employees took a serious spill and needed to be taken to the hospital, I stayed with him. Once he was treated, I saw him home. I'd been up all night, wasn't in great shape, and when I got to the piazza, I saw a man and woman by the Florian, deep in conversation. It didn't seem right to interrupt, and I had your itinerary, so I knew I'd be able to meet up with you later on. At La Calcina, remember? We got off to a rough start because my timing was wrong and I was annoyed with myself. But things smoothed out, and I thought . . . . It should have been *me*!" He stared at my slightly protruding tummy and shook his head. "*I* was the one who was supposed to meet you that morning."

"You . . . "

"Josie ran the personal, screened the responses, and told me I was perfect for you. She sent me your schedule, and suggested I meet you at sunrise in the piazza."

"But Michael, why on earth didn't you tell me?"

"Like I said, Josie didn't want trouble. And I didn't realize that this misunderstanding was keeping you and Max apart. Maybe I didn't *want* to realize. But I care deeply about you, Claire, and want your happiness. It's been very tough keeping this all from you. Finally, my conscience got the better of me and I want to come clean."

"Then I had it all wrong, blaming Max for something he had no part in." I had been guilty of holding everyone around me to impossible standards.

"I know. I'm sorry." He looked down at his shoes.

I thought of a long-ago conversation with Max when I repeated Daniela's story about the marchesa and how she wanted to be the woman most often portrayed by artists.

"You know which character is most often portrayed in the movies?" Max had asked..

"Jesus Christ?"

"Sherlock Holmes."

And I was the bumbling Watson.

I thanked Michael for telling me about the personal, and as soon as we parted, I called Max. He wasn't answering, so I left a message explaining my confusion about the ad and our meeting in the piazza. I had jumped to conclusions, and I apologized for my stubborn foolishness. *Mea culpa, mea culpa.* I told him I missed him. Still, I stopped short of letting him know about the baby. I needed to be sure first that everything was right between the two of us. I wasn't a Venetian painter who thought on canvas; I needed to reflect before loading my brush with paint.

It was February, *corto e maledetto*, short and cursed, but not in Venice, not during Carnevale. I received no response to my heartfelt apology. I had forgiven Michael, if in fact there was anything to forgive, because I understood his dilemma. He and I continued to spend time together, enjoying the festivities of Carnevale, roaming the alleys and squares filled with revelers wearing hawk-like masks of leather and pressed paper that protruded from enveloping cloaks. The city was so thick with *la nebbia*, the fog, that lookouts were needed in the boats that disappeared into the opaque distance.

In the piazza, a huge screen propped against the Campanile displayed Benetton and Coke ads, and Bellini drinks were sold from a large tent.

"Doesn't matter how well they're disguised, the Japanese tourists give themselves away by bowing whenever anyone takes their picture," said Michael. He looked dashing in his black cloak and sequined mask.

I admired him from behind my feathered mask. My deep purple cloak prompted him to say, "You look more mysterious than ever, little violet." He took my hand. "And I don't want to lose you." I felt a rush of desire for him, felt myself open up to the possibility of falling in love with him. Bernie had never really been present, and neither it seemed was Max. Doubts and questions began to stir. Had I avoided any attachment with Michael because he was the first love interest in my life to be truly emotionally available? And did his availability make the relationship more frightening because the stakes were higher? If the relationship failed, I would never be able to say that it was because he wasn't there for me. And in a way, we had met by chance, on the *vaporetto*, an encounter that Michael didn't remember because he was so focused on having missed his appointed meeting in the piazza earlier that morning.

"Now who is this little violet?" A spectacular couple approached us, the woman wearing a Mona Lisa mask and the man dressed as Leonardo da Vinci. I recognized the warmth in the voice, the silver hair, and the diamonds on the slender hand curled in the crook of the man's elbow.

"Daniela. And Chef." After embracing each of them, I introduced them to Michael. What expression Daniela might be wearing behind her mask I could only guess; she acted as if encountering Michael and me hand-in-hand was the most natural thing in the world.

The four of us bought *fritole*, fried balls of dough with pieces of dried fruit and pine nuts and sprinkled with sugar. We drank hot, spiced wine served to us by a young man called Gabri, dressed in gold lamé. It was the end of his shift, and Carlo Massini showed up to join him. He introduced himself to Chef and Michael and gave Daniela and me each a kiss on the cheek. Then the six of us left the piazza together to wander the *calli*.

"This year's program is *Invisible Cities*," Carlo said, as we all made our way along Strada Nova, "Calvino's book about Marco Polo's conversations with Kublai Khan about the fantastic cities he's seen on his travels." We stopped to watch a fire-eater, steady on his widespread feet, exhaling slowly as the flame that rose upward neared his open mouth for quick extinguishing.

"Each time they meet, he describes an imaginary city suspended between memory and desire," Carlo said.

"Past and future," said Gabri. "The city called 'Zora' holds precious things we want to remember."

We popped into a church whose door read, NO MASKS INSIDE. I smiled when I noticed that Gabri had taken Carlo's hand. After each of us lit candles, we returned to Strada Nova and continued to the stage set for a museum that held a crystal globe in each of its rooms.

"Each globe holds an ideal city," Gabri said. "But by the time the city is constructed, it has already changed."

Like Cornell's little worlds that stand still while the planet continues to spin. I imagined the soul as a city filled with memory palaces reached by traveling the uneven terrain of the heart. These days my dream of a life together with Max felt as static as the mummified waves in Cornell's *Roses des Vents*, like something to be preserved in a bottle, along with a feather or a boat ticket. It was a fantasy of mine that morning in the piazza to be whisked away by a wild romantic love, but every day since, life moved on, shifting like the Grand Canal with its boat traffic and tides. Moments like this dislodged me from my old, familiar thought patterns, my self-sabotaging techniques. I felt myself growing from within as Michael's warm hand continued to hold mine loosely enough so that I didn't feel smothered and tightly enough so that I felt safe. He wasn't past or future. He was present tense.

He and Daniela were engaged in an animated conversation about books, in particular, those at the Libreria Acqua Alta. Chef and Gabri were comparing recipes for *fritoli*. Carlo and I shared tips about the art of collage.

When we parted in the wee hours of the morning, Michael took me in his arms, lifted my chin with his finger until our eyes met, and gave me a long, lingering kiss. The deep feeling I had for him had grown slowly, steadily. My body felt an unexpected rush of desire and longing for him, and I dreamed of staying in his arms forever. Love and bliss for those who kiss under the Bridge of Sighs.

A week later, the six of us met for lunch at the Londra. Arriving early, I retreated to the hotel's reading room to settle into a cozy sofa by the fire and admire framed copies of Tchaikovsky's sheet music. I hummed a few notes and heard the faintest of creaks on the cushion beside me.

"Music was my refuge," the composer said in a soft voice, "born of my darkest moments." Tchaikovsky's hair was tousled—his dark eyes bore into me as he explained, "I tried to link myself with women. But that only led to disaster, tormented as I was by my preference for men. Soon after my wedding, I attempted to drown myself." He sobbed, his face in his hands. "That melody from my Fourth Symphony." He looked up at me, his face wet with tears. "It begins with gloom, but in the finale, I discover the light." His face brightened for a moment before he began to weep once more. "Open yourself to the possibility of happiness and prepare to accept it." His message was one of hope, but he looked so terribly sad.

"There, there," I said, and as I patted his back—*piano, pianissimo*—the anger toward Bernie dissolved in my chest, like a sugar cube in hot tea. The composer dabbed at his nose with a lace-edged hankie and left me. Nothing remained but a faint indentation on the cushion, a suggestion of spicy cologne in the air, and a sensation of lightness that comes with letting go of a long-held grudge.

"Gabri's apartment is on the Giudecca Canal," Carlo said, "with a *vaporetto* stop on either side." He rolled his eyes.

"Noisy?" said Chef.

"You wouldn't believe," said Carlo.

"Diesels set off a vibration that rattles the windows," Gabri said. "When we stuffed newspaper in the cracks, we found articles lodged there that dated back to the fall of Mussolini!"

Sometimes when I was caught off guard, memories of Max still rattled my windows. Ever since Michael confessed to answering the ad, I felt foolish and guilty. Weeks ago, I was more than happy to jump to conclusions, whip myself into a frenzy, and make choices based on false premises when, in fact, Max and I had met by chance after all.

"I never noticed those mountains in the distance," I said, taking in the view. "They look like a ruined castle."

"We see them only in winter because of the refraction of light," Daniela said. "But the Dolomites are always there."

"*Certo*," said Chef.

Some things are always with us whether or not they are visible. Just yesterday, the café's orchestra was playing "I'll Be Seeing You," and in Venice I saw Max on the bridge when a mother struggled with her carriage, I saw him standing by Marini's angel as I cruised past the Guggenheim, and when I wandered into the Ghetto, he was there, in the upstairs window. But I didn't hear a word from him, and our times together had become faded snapshots in an album whose pages had been turned.

When I announced to everyone at the table that I was pregnant, Carlo's eyes widened, Daniela and Chef exchanged smiles, and Gabri offered his congratulations. As Michael took my hand under the table and squeezed it, the conversation turned briefly to plans for the baby, the due date, and the state of my health.

Then Carlo passed around his latest photographs. He was playing around with color and superimposed images that resulted in a dreamy effect. They were a big hit with Chef, who asked if Carlo would be willing to photograph some of his favorite dishes at the Gritti for an updated brochure. The six of us sat comfortably through the meal and dessert, like the oldest and best of friends.

February led to March. I wrote Bernie a letter wishing him happiness with his new family and sending along some gift-wrapped onesies and baby socks. I couldn't resist sharing my good news, all in caps. I'M EXPECTING A BABY!

Josie wrote to say that the café in Newburyport was going splendidly and that Boccaccio had made himself at home, entertaining the patrons with his pearls of wisdom. In fact, she and Ethan had decided to name the place Boccaccio's Café.

Michael went to Rome, hired on a temporary basis to oversee the men's department.

Daniela called to say she was in town for an appointment with an author, but she had time to meet me at the Florian for brunch. She talked about her latest projects and asked about mine.

"And you know, I've decided to follow through with a suggestion you made in Paris," I told her as we ate our sandwiches. "About the spirits. I'm baking them cookies."

"You've had enough of them?"

"Let's just say that Tchaikovsky pretty much wrapped things up for me."

"You're comfortable now in your own skin."

I nodded. "By the way, where's Zola?"

"Getting a shampoo. In fact," she said, checking her watch, "I really must be going." She kissed me on each cheek. "I'll call you tomorrow."

On Strada Nova, I stopped at Boscolo's and studied the multitude of sweets in the window: *baci di gondoliere, baci d'alassio, baci di dama*. Kisses, all kinds of kisses. I stepped inside to ask if I could borrow the signora's pattern for the

Saint Martin cookie. When she hesitated, I explained that this was an unusual circumstance, that I had an obligation to make these cookies for a few special friends, just this once. "I promise I'll take very good care of the pattern," I said.

"I have no need for it in the month of March," she said agreeably.

That afternoon I baked the Saint Martin cookies and, once they cooled, I frosted them with tinted royal icing, and finished them off with sprinkles, nonpareils, jimmies, foil wrapped chocolates, and silver dragées. I wrapped and labeled a cookie for each of my spectral buddies—Byron, Marcel, Jacopo, and the rest of the gang. Then, basket in hand, I walked along the Canal toward my first destination, the piazza.

A produce boat went by, sitting low in the water. Two gondoliers chatting at one of the landing docks—Franco and Angelo—interrupted their conversation to wave and shout to me, then they called to the passengers in a small motorboat. Sitting at the rudder was the silver-haired Chef, all bundled up with his hair ruffling in the breeze, and facing him, a terrier sitting in a red sweater, one paw on the throttle. Daniela, wearing a kerchief, sat in the stern. She turned to me and smiled. Meant for each other, I thought, waving and blowing kisses until the boat disappeared from view. Then I continued my walk around the mist-muffled city, delivering cookies to hotels, museums, and cafés, to each spot where I had encountered a ghost.

Not long ago, I had been a globetrotting beggar searching for my place in the world, not a satin-stitched heart on a pillow or a red pushpin on a map, but a real place that I could point to and say, "That's where I belong." The spirits sensed my desire and showed up to share their Saint Martin capes with me— their pain, their wisdom. They were beggars, too, in need of my ear, and my company. But now it was time to thank them and move on.

22

Dai e dai la barca ariva ai pai
Row and row until the boat reaches the poles

In Venice, the cactus blooms in December and the tourists burst forth in April when the first rendition of "O Sole Mio" is heard on the Canal, when fireflies and wild roses fill the courtyards, when the Rialto overflows with asparagus and golden apples, and when boats haul everything from sofas to chandeliers along the Canal in preparation for summer guests.

Encounters with tourists were not always pleasant. Just this morning, an inspector writing up a passenger on the *Numero Uno* explained, "When the office is closed, you must buy your ticket on the boat. The signs on the platforms . . . " The tourist's cell phone rang and, ignoring him, she took the call. He threw up his hands. "You will remain on board until everyone else gets off, and you will pay." Meanwhile, a Venetian politely told another visitor that smoking was not permitted onboard. "Oh, really?" the man said and rubbed his cigarette out on the gunnel. Then he moved to the other side and lit up again.

I visited the Frari, a Gothic church smaller than its model, San Giovanni e Paolo, and containing fewer dead doges. What it did have was an incredible Titian. In a revolutionary move, the artist placed the Virgin off to one side rather than front and center. A boy stands on the knee of his mother playing with her veil and twisting around while she's trying to concentrate on the saints gathered around them. This work by Titian pulled me in more than Bellini's altarpiece in the Sacristy where an enthroned Madonna, grave, sweet, and otherworldly, holds her steadfast baby son.

I rested my hand on my tummy and felt myself moving away from Bellini's vision of a quiet, ideal motherhood and toward that portrayed by Titian, a less perfect and more dramatic, more expansive motherhood. Bellini's lovely painting became for me a static model in a glass globe. Motherhood was not going to be perfect. My baby was going to tug at things. My baby would twist and turn and be very much alive and of this world.

At the Rialto I bought bright red cherries and plums called *gocche d'oro*, drops of gold, to arrange along with white peaches and green figs in a bowl on my table. Isabella called that morning, asking if she could bring over some homemade soup. I set two places and, when she arrived, ladled out the soup, thick with chicken, onions, and parsley and fragrant with vermouth. I added freshly ground pepper and grated Parmesan cheese, and poured her some wine.

"And what is this?" I said, taking a spoonful. "Bacon?"

"An unexpected ingredient, but we're secular Jews, you know."

"Delicious."

"I wanted to talk with you face to face, Claire." I put my spoon down. "Carlo has told us that you are expecting a baby. Perhaps Max's baby."

"It's true," I said, searching her eyes for a hidden agenda.

Isabella and I proceeded to have a long heart-to-heart about my feelings towards Max, as well as my misgivings and misapprehensions. I didn't want to ruin his career, I told her. I didn't think he would want the baby. And I didn't think he would want me. Not now.

"Give him a chance, Claire. *El xe on toco de pan.* He's as good as a loaf of bread—as good as gold." I asked her not to tell Max about the baby. I would do that myself when the time was right.

While Pierre traveled with Yuan-Lin's party on the Silk Road expedition, Nicole spent time in my apartment visiting with me and avoiding what she called the *bagno di folla*, the noisy crowd-bath taking place in the alleys and squares and on the canals. She thumbed through the alphabet book that I had nearly finished. "Bubbling of a fountain, Coo of a pigeon," she read to Françoise, who reclined in her baby chair on the tabletop while I brewed us a pot of tea. "Splash of oars, Throb of the diesel engines." Françoise had dozed off. "The collages are *très beaux*, Claire, and your captions are superb."

"Oh Nicole, you're too kind," I said. "How's Pierre doing?"

"He travels sometimes on camel back, eating goat's head soup, but believe me, it is not all hardship." She took two sugar cubes and dropped them in her tea. "He sent me digital postcards from a hotel styled after a Ming dynasty palace and writes about its quiet courtyards, hour-long foot massages, views of the Gobi Desert. He's seen the Crescent Moon Lake at sunrise and the Caves of the Thousand Buddhas."

"He must miss you, though."

She drew a long breath. "Yes, but he's living his dream." And Max was living his.

"Are you living yours, Nicole?" Was I living mine?

Smiling, she gave Françoise a kiss on her chubby cheek. "Is there any doubt?" Maybe not for Nicole, but for me, misgivings moved in like the fog and tendrils of doubt crept along the alleyways of my heart.

I went home and finished my work on the Madonna paintings. It was true what Daniela said about the Venetians viewing Mary as one of their own. Mary, never static or stiff, would half close her eyes as if to ward off sorrow, or she would stare unblinking, waiting stoically for what was to come. She was peaceful and mysterious, or vulnerable and beseeching. She gazed at her child, pulled us into her thoughts, stood bravely, or fell in a limp heap. She was a wonder worker often seated in a church of golden mosaics, accompanied by lilies for virtue, turtledoves for love, myrtle for constancy, pearls for continuity, or a parrot (greatly resembling Boccaccio, I might add) of outspokenness.

Finally, I heard from Max. "I'm sorry I couldn't call sooner, but I've been really busy and I lost my cell phone."

"I'm glad you're all right. I phoned you ages ago and left a message. You never got it?"

"No, no messages."

"I discovered that Josie ran a personal ad for me. I thought that's how you and I met, and the thought of you two colluding and keeping me in the dark really bothered me. I felt deceived and wondered why you weren't telling me about it. But it was all a crazy mix-up, and I made too much of it. I'm so sorry."

"Well, I don't know anything about a personal ad, but I'm glad it's all straightened out. And really, I don't see what difference it would have made. I plan to come to Venice as soon as I finish with things here."

"When will that be?"

"A week or two. I have some loose ends to tie up at Haifa."

"I can't wait to see you."

"Me, too."

Josie arrived from the States for a weeklong visit, leaving Ethan at home to run the coffee shop. It was raining a cold drizzle when she came bounding up my steps, wielding an umbrella decorated in large, bright red poppies. "Claire, you look so beautiful!" she said, shaking off the rain. She left the open umbrella on the doormat and handed me a gift of velvet *furlane*, the traditional slippers worn by gondoliers. A beautiful garnet color and with rubber soles, they felt heavenly when I slipped them on my swollen feet.

She settled into the kitchen while I made her coffee. "Love this," she said, looking through my alphabet book. "It's very sweet, Claire," she said, closing the book gently. "And how is Max?"

"Doing well. Coming back soon, he says."

She nodded. "That's good. And Michael?"

"Oh, we've been having the best time . . . " And I went on to describe our lunches, picture taking, and visits to the bookstore, as Josie studied my face.

By nighttime, the sky had cleared. Daniela invited Josie and me for a drink beneath the stars at the Gritti. She hugged me, finding it difficult to encircle my girth.

"Keep my friend far away from Ramo Salizzado Zustro," she told Josie, referring to the narrowest street in the city. "Less than a meter wide. If Claire gets wedged in there, we'll never get her out!"

"This is the most beautiful place," Josie said, looking around. "I miss not living here." Zola positioned herself over my feet, warming them. "The good news is I'm collecting air miles." She sipped her brandy.

Daniela inquired about Max. "He's fine," I said.

"And things between you?"

"I really need to see him. It's been too long."

Daniela looked thoughtful as she watched the boats drift up and down the Grand Canal.

Then Josie said, "You know, I don't remember all the details, but the response to that personal ad? In his note, the guy described himself as 'present-tense.' I wasn't sure what that meant, but it sounded good." I sipped my tea. She wanted to be let off the hook. "He signed off with the initial 'M.' Anyway, when I sent him your itinerary, I promised he wouldn't be disappointed."

"Love has a most unpredictable itinerary," Daniela said, finishing her brandy. She gave Zola's leash a gentle tug. "It's good to see you both, but I need to say my goodbyes, as I'm expected at the Massinis'."

"I know that 'M' stood for Michael," I said, when Daniela was gone. "Not Max. Michael confessed that you two made a pact to keep it quiet."

"So now you know."

"I was angry with you for a long time. All this confusion was so needless. If only you hadn't run that damned ad . . . "

"It did turn out well, admit it." Josie's face held an expectant look. The ad brought Michael into my life. Thoughts of him made me feel as if I were wearing a soft wool sweater. I remembered our Wednesday conversations about anything and everything, including our deepest feelings and fears.

Josie and I left the Gritti arm in arm. We walked along the south edge of the island and bought *gianduiotto da passaggio*, big cups of fluffy whipped cream with slabs of hazelnut chocolate gelato.

"This is terrific." Josie waved her dainty plastic spoon at a jogger who ran by with his tiny dog. She took another bite. "Mmm. This tastes a lot like Nutella." She licked her lips.

Back in my kitchen, we tried a new recipe—*panna cotta*, a silky egg custard topped with a honey paste. "Cooking is like love," Josie said, "to be entered into with abandon, or not at all." And with that, she added an unauthorized splash of cognac. That was Josie. She never changes.

When she left for Newburyport, I wrote to Max, describing my life in Venice and my book about the sounds of the city—the sweeping sound of brooms in the piazza, a student practicing the violin, the jouncing of the postman's wheels as he pulled his cart up the stone stairs—and footsteps, always footsteps. With different shoes and rhythms, Venetians could recognize their friends from the next alley over.

Max wrote about his life in Israel, his new friends.

One early afternoon, I sat on a wrought-iron bench in the park near my apartment, warming myself in the April sun and trying to ignore a deep ache that ran the length of my legs and another that circumscribed my heart. On the corner, a vendor was hawking roses for *El Zorno del Bocolo*, the special day a man presents his beloved with a red rose. According to legend, a valiant knight mortally wounded while fighting during a crusade, has a friend deliver a white rose to his darling, but because he has held the rose to his wounded heart, the rose turns red.

A stray petal floated in the air and landed on the bench beside me. My baby wasn't kicking much now. I needed to run to the bathroom often and sometimes had trouble breathing because everything was getting crowded inside me. But sitting there on the bench, I grew more comfortable and content. Every time I daydreamed about the baby, it was Michael I saw cradling the infant, singing to it, rocking it. Nicole came down and joined me. She asked me to hold Françoise while she rummaged for a bottle. The baby's eyes rolled beneath pale blue lids. While her fingers with tiny nails curled around my forefinger, her pursed lips held an iridescent bubble that expanded and contracted with her breathing.

Clouds gathered, and Nicole invited me up to her apartment to make *zuppa primaverile* with fresh peas, spinach, leeks, and asparagus tips cooked in tarragon broth. Soon Etienne came home from school and sniffed approvingly of the green soup before starting his homework.

"Our class is reviewing the history of the city," he said, unfolding a map on the kitchen table. "I like the way my teacher describes the map of Venice. Hand in hand. See?"

I *couldn't* see it until he traced the landforms with his finger and the image of the two clasped hands became clear.

"I've always heard Venice described as a fish," I said.

"But I like this better, no? Cannaregio is here, the knuckles on the top hand." And the Grand Canal, an inverted blue S-shaped line, defined where the two hands touched.

"Nicer than a fish," I said, staring at the image.

When I returned home, it was dark and drizzling, and as I opened the door to my apartment, the phone was ringing. It was Max, struggling to keep the excitement from his voice. "I'm arriving early tomorrow morning. Meet me in the piazza, at sunrise?"

Outside, the rain spattered against the windows, blurring the view below and turning the walkway silvery-white. My thoughts returned to that early morning in the piazza and the vulnerability I had felt as a woman discarded for a man. When Max arrived, young, bright, and enthusiastic, a powerful jolt passed between us. How long had it been since someone had flirted with me? I couldn't remember. I'd fallen in love on the spot, head over heels with— possibility. My ego was momentarily restored, but later, darker emotions crept in: familiar feelings of jealousy, insecurity, and unworthiness, the same sadness and longing linked to my days spent with Bernie, when I was left wondering why I wasn't enough.

Until now, I hadn't considered the similarities between the two men, their self-absorption and emotional distancing. Ironically, these conditions may have been their major attraction because if Bernie and Max didn't have much to give, then I didn't have much to lose. The rain continued to plink methodically on the roof as if to drive the point home. It didn't matter whether there had been a personal ad or not; this was more about wanting something so badly that, no matter how inauthentic, I tried to make it fit. That's where the question of authenticity came into play. "Max is young," I said aloud to the rhythm of the rain on the roof. "He doesn't want marriage, and he doesn't want a baby." And once I put it into words, I recognized it as the truth. But this was his baby, too, and he had a right to participate as much or as little as he wanted.

I thought about how Michael made me feel and who I was when we were together. Everything was so easy and comfortable. He was tender and forgiving, accepting of imperfections. His being "present tense" had at first sounded pretentious, but Michael truly lived in the moment, not allowing himself to be haunted by the past and not worrying about the future.

In the morning, I packed a thermos of hot chocolate and biscotti. Leaving the apartment, I met a tawny cat, the same one that slept below the easel at the Madonna dell'Orto. She was fat with kittens, and slinking through the dark alley. She meowed at me in recognition, rubbed against my leg, and purring, continued on her way.

I passed between the columns of the *piazzetta* and turned the corner to see that two chairs had been pulled from the stack at the Florian. A man sat in one of the chairs, a man balancing a cup on his knee.

23

Quando la pera è matura, casca da sè.
When the pear is ripe, it will fall on its own.

"Claire?" Max rose from his feet as I approached him, and stared at me open mouthed. "You look so . . . different." New hairstyle, new clothes, and then as his eyes traveled down the length of my body, "What's happened?"

"I wanted to tell you in person, Max," I said. "The night of the flood? You know, all that talk about Ruskin."

"You're sure, Claire?" His face filled with alarm, and he turned slightly as if he were making ready to run down a dark alley. He looked so young.

Sure? Sure of what, that I was expecting a baby or that it happened the night of the *acqua alta*? "I know it's a shock, but I thought it would be better if you finished your work at Haifa without having to worry about . . . " With a sweeping motion, I indicated my condition, "this. Now that you're here, we'll have time to talk."

I settled in a chair, poured myself some hot chocolate, and offered some to him. I felt a little sorry for him as he held his empty cup out, clutching it with both hands. "To meet like this in the piazza," I said, pouring the hot chocolate. "You're such a romantic."

I thought back to that morning in November, his enthusiasm about Saint Mark's and the architecture, his quoting from my book. I was getting the impression that Max was more child-like than ever, a kid returned from summer camp, and that it was possible to end up with two children on my hands, the baby and Max.

We met by chance and, like the man and woman in Giorgione's *Tempest*, were unaware of what loomed around us. Then we were hit by the thunderbolt. Weren't we? The dramatic atmosphere overcame us, and although there was a river separating us, I'd seen that bridge in the background, flimsy, yet it was there. Like the man and woman in the painting, Max and I remained apart and the bridge *was* flimsy.

"I don't know what to say," Max said. "You were globetrotting, and I wanted a flexible lifestyle. I thought we'd pick up where we left off, but . . . "

"But I've settled down, Max. Made a home for myself. The books I'm working on are a great alternative to all that travel. My life has changed."

"Picture books. Hmm." He sipped the hot chocolate, as if to stall.

"It's not so bad, is it? Living in the most beautiful city in the world. Bringing up a baby in a place where babies are adored."

"Maybe for *you*, but it's not exactly the dream I had in mind."

"No. No, of course not."

We talked for a long time. We decided that I would stay in Venice for now and that Max could come and go as he pleased, pursue his studies, and play a significant part in our baby's life, or not. Dreams. I dreamed of a man that I would care for and desire. In Venice, I had been searching for the perfect mirror in which to see myself; it wasn't the ideal man that eluded me. During my time here, I had discovered my true self and slipped into it, and it became clear that Max and I were not meant for each other. I didn't want to compromise my happiness for someone who didn't share my values and my dreams. Not when I knew in my heart that there was someone who viewed the world through my same lens.

My spirits lifted as my heart filled with the certainty that everything would be as it should be. It is true that the rising sun affects a thousand other things, but here it set the piazza aglow, as though it had nothing else in the universe to do.

Max scribbled his updated contact information on a sticky note and handed it to me, his expression sober.

"Don't worry, Max. I'm so happy to be having this baby, and I'm certain things will work out for all of us."

When he put his cheek to mine and said, "I'll keep in touch," his familiar fragrance of deep winter woods penetrated my thoughts. Years ago, my friends and I were skating on a frozen pond, playing "snap the whip," and I was on the tail end. As we skated faster and faster, the centrifugal force became so great that I lost my grip and went flying into the woods where, startled, a fawn and its mother rose from the leaves and stood alert, staring at me. Mittens to face, I arrived airborne, landing in a heap on the cold ground. I got a little scratched and bruised, but it was worth it, to let go like that. Venice was as good a place as any to let go. I felt relief as Max and I parted at the Florian and went our separate ways.

Then I heard a pigeon stir and coo, and the sound of familiar footsteps moving across the piazza. A middle-aged man approached, his strong chin jutting forward, his high forehead glowing in the morning light, his purposeful walk resounding on the cobblestones. The hard line of his square shoulders was outlined in soft wool, his strong hands cupped loosely at his sides. Yes, he was coming straight toward me, and *el me piaxe. Yes, he pleases me.*

Heavenly Panna Cotta

4 cups half-and-half
1/2 cup plus 2 tablespoons granulated sugar
2 teaspoons vanilla extract
Oil (enough to oil the ramekins)
4 1/2 teaspoons powdered gelatin
6 tablespoons cold water
Chestnut honey or vincotta for garnish

Heat the half-and-half and sugar in a saucepan until the sugar is dissolved.
Remove from heat and stir in the vanilla extract.
Lightly oil eight ramekins.
Sprinkle the gelatin over the cold water in a medium-sized bowl and let stand 10 minutes.

Pour the very warm cream mixture over the gelatin and stir until the gelatin is completely dissolved.

Divide the panna cotta mixture into ramekins and chill until firm, at least four hours or, better yet, overnight.

Run a sharp knife around the edge of each panna cotta and unmold it onto a serving plate. Before serving, drizzle with warm chestnut honey or a few drops of vincotta, a dark, dense, sweet grape must.

And why not? Add an unauthorized splash of cognac!

ACKNOWLEDGMENTS

I offer a special thanks to my daughter, Caitlin Wright, my inspiration;

To The Fine Arts Work Center, Provincetown, Massachusetts, and my teachers: Amy Bloom, Michael Cunningham, Maria Flook, Michael Klein, and Margot Livesey;

To members of the Murfreesboro Writers Group;

And to those friends and relations, and various readers of earlier drafts of the manuscript: Joy Johannessen, Susan M. Ashley, Laura Stout LaTour, Lynne Barrett, Stephen Outten, Lee Rennick, Deb Simpson, and Bob Fish.

I am especially grateful to June Hall McCash for reading the final draft and for offering her support and encouragement, to D. Michelle Adkerson for her careful editing, and to Nora Hibbard for finalizing this project and making it the best book possible.

This novel is informed by my enjoyment of a wealth of books, stories, and films. The following sources have been influential and indispensable:

Calvino, Italo. *Invisible Cities.* [*Le città invisibili.*] Torino: Giulio Einaudi Editore, 1972.
Larson, Gary. *The Complete Far Side.* Kansas City: Andrews McMeel, 2003.
Morris, James. *The World of Venice.* New York: Harcourt, 1974.
Morris, Jan. Foreword to "*The Harry's Bar Cookbook,*" by Arrigo Cipriani. New York: Bantam Dell, 1991.
Ryersson, Scot D., and Michael Orlando Yaccarino. *Infinite Variety: The Life and Legend of the Marchesa Casati.* Minneapolis: University of Minnesota Press, 2004.
Soloman, Deborah. *Utopia Parkway: The Life and Work of Joseph Cornell.* New York: Farrar, Straus and Giroux, 1997.
Stewart, Susan. *On Longing.* Baltimore: Johns Hopkins University Press, 1984.
Waldman, Diane. *Joseph Cornell, Master of Dreams.* New York: Harry N. Abrams, 1977.

And especially for *Dark Side of the Church.* New York: Palgrave Macmillan, 2008, by my late husband, Robert Michael.

For a full bibliography, please visit my website: susanashleymichael.com.

CPSIA information can be obtained at www.ICGtesting.com
Printed in the USA
BVOW010805010212

281904BV00003B/97/P